Yellow Pages
a catalogue of intentions

Yellow Pages

a catalogue of intentions

Nicole Markotić

Red Deer College Press

Copyright © 1995 Nicole Markotić
All rights reserved. No part of this book may be
reproduced by any means, electronic or mechanical,
including photography, recording, or any information
and retrieval system, without permission in writing
from the publisher.

THE PUBLISHERS
Red Deer College Press
56 Avenue & 32 Street Box 5005
Red Deer Alberta Canada T4N 5H5

CREDITS
Cover Art by Alex Murchison
Cover Design by Gordon Robertson
Text Design by Dennis Johnson
Printed and Bound in Canada by Parkland
ColourPress Ltd for Red Deer College Press

ACKNOWLEDGMENTS
Financial support provided by the Alberta Founda-
tion for the Arts, a beneficiary of the Lottery Fund
of the Government of Alberta, and by the Canada
Council, the Department of Canadian Heritage and
Red Deer College.

COMMITTED TO THE DEVELOPMENT OF CULTURE AND THE ARTS

CANADIAN CATALOGUING IN PUBLICATION DATA
Markotić, Nicole.
Yellow pages
ISBN 0-88995-132-2
1. Bell, Alexander Graham, 1847–1922—Fiction. I. Title.
PS8576.A74Y4 1995   C813'.54   C94-910898-7
PR9199.3.M37Y4 1995

Contents

This book is dedicated to Winnipeg and its impossible inhabitants—who understand the magical properties of Confusion Corner and gelati in winter.

I would like to acknowledge financial and academic support from the University of Manitoba, especially the English Department, during much of the writing of this book.

As well, I would like to thank the following people for their generous pen markings and other feats of dedication: Méira Cook, Rosemary Deckert Nixon, Lorraine, Michelle, and Roland Markotić, Suzette Mayr and Margaret Sweatman.

Finally, I wish to express special thanks to Robert Kroetsch—for his famous unanswerable questions and his endless complaints that I had too many characters, not enough characters, that I didn't know what a character was, sometimes, yet who still managed to expect brilliant words from me in the most generously demanding way; for getting impatient and for being unbelievably patient; for prescribing narrative rather than biography, fiction rather than history; and for insisting this was (still) a good idea and of course I could write it.

And to Aritha van Herk—for her famous and fearsome red pen; for never letting me take the easy way (even when that seemed such a seductive route); for a friendship that includes bad movies and crab apple escapes; and for dreaming concern onto the page and then leaving it there.

–Nicole Markotić

To love someone is to love that person's body and language.
—ABDELKEBIR KHATIBI
Love in Two Languages

All history is contemporary history: not in the ordinary sense of the word, where contemporary history means the history of the comparatively recent past, but in the strict sense: the consciousness of one's own activity as one actually performs it.
—R.G. COLLINGWOOD
The Idea of History

I would rather be remembered as a teacher of the deaf than as the telephone's inventor.
—ALEXANDER GRAHAM BELL

I

~~~~~~

Automatons that Travel London

ALECK'S NAMESAKE, ALEXANDER THE GREAT, invented a telephone.

He was the first in a parade of inventors stretching to the nineteenth century. Through a gigantic double-ringed horn, a loudspeaker, he shouted military orders and yelled formation maneuvers. He stood on the summit of a hill and threw his voice at men standing twelve miles away. This mechanical device amplified vibrations released from his throat. He threw his voice around like he was passing out loaves and fishes. The trick he never accomplished was himself hearing this trick. He was deaf to his own magnification.

Aleck, growing into his namesake's name, decides he will hear his own magnificence. Decides he must stop the cycle of invention. Must become the final installment in a long line of telephone inventors. A process of invention that begins with one Alexander and completes with another. Aleck will be remembered. Aleck's voice will reverberate into the future. Aleck will stop the chain of invention. If Aleck will be last.

ALECK ENTERS the world as a birthday present for his grandfather. The two Alexanders share a name and a birth date. They share the same curved earlobes. They share perfect enunciation. Grandfather Alexander had been a shoemaker who longed for the notoriety of the stage. He spent years as a prompter, staring at actors' feet, hissing up at them to recite forgotten lines he could see clearly written on his prompter's page. No theater fan knew his face. When he quit, he opened a school for elocution, taught sons of noble Scots how to pronounce the King's English. Shakespeare and Dickens. Grandfather Alexander could recite Dickens better than Dickens, but he attracted smaller audiences.

SUMMERS, Aleck visits Grandfather Alexander at his retirement home in London. His grandfather hustles him off to a tailor and buys Aleck a proper suit and coat and top hat. Mortified, Aleck wears his costume everywhere in the hopes it will wear out by the time he returns to Edinburgh. The tweeds scratch his legs and sound like a cat licking fur. Grandfather expects Aleck to learn how to walk so that his clothes wear out evenly. So that his clothes settle into a proper fitting. Aleck feels like a dandy. His small chest sweats beneath sweater and vest and jacket. The suit hums and rubs a continuous rustle. His grandfather's voice reverberates inside the top hat. Quite right. Round your vowels. Heads up. Aleck balances layers of conversations above his head; he tilts his neck to see if the words leak out. Aleck learns to walk his grandfather's walk, learns to fit his body to these clothes. Ears at attention, Aleck curls his fingers around Grandfather's handsome cane. He no longer runs across the yellow grass but strolls along swept pathways.

BACK IN EDINBURGH, Aleck decides to grow out of his nickname. Melly taunts him with *lick* and *lock* and *lack*. Aleck wants a name to fit his adult walk, stylish and mature. He can't demand they use his birth name while his grandfather's still alive. Families who name their children after themselves find shortcuts to avoid confusion, and Aleck doesn't want just another nickname. He hauls out the dictionary and looks up famous men: Chopin, Liszt, Mendelssohn. He needs to consider rhythm. His name begins—Alexander—with four syllables and ends—Bell—with one. The middle name Aleck will adopt must contain two. Or three. Lucky. Sailor. Governor.

Aleck's father believes in Canada. Canada is a mythical country where you get better if you're sick, where you learn to breathe again after your lungs have collapsed. Aleck's father exchanges Christmas cards with a Canadian friend, Graham. A friend he met when he himself was sick and sent to Canada to recover. A friend who has transformed into letters and postage stamps. Every year, Graham postpones a visit to Edinburgh, promising: next year.

Aleck meets the name years before he meets the person.

Then, without any letter of warning, Graham-from-Canada knocks casually on the Bell front door, no one expecting the visit. Once I write a plan down, I'm already too bored to follow through, Graham explains. He took a boat from Newfoundland to sip tea with his friends in their kitchen. I've got to get back tomorrow, he apologizes, traveling takes so long.

Aleck trails this invisible friend made flesh, trying out his name on his own tongue. He likes that it starts with a *grrrr*. He likes that the Canadian spelling alters the Scottish *Graeme*. Because Canada is my destiny, he tells Melly, who spits on the grass in response. Melly wants them to stay Melly and Aleck, but that's not possible. Graham Bell, Graham Bell, Graham Bell, Aleck yells at Melly. Their father's guest turns back just as he reaches the street, then turns away again, leaving his name behind in Aleck's mouth.

ALECK INHERITS music from his mother. Eliza hears less and less every day, and Aleck more and more. He sweats nights from an incessant beat-beat in his ears and wakes up delirious. The only relief is while he makes music. Aleck takes lessons from Signor Auguste Benoit Bertini. Hammers at the keys until Bach, Beethoven, Mozart crowd his veins. Hours and hours of staring at black-and-white notation, making it mean music. Eliza sits by her son's side, sets the mouthpiece of her hearing apparatus on the piano's sounding board. So she can see the sound, so she can feel notes her own fingers no longer inspire. Aleck pounds and pounds, his blood's pulse living in his fingers, his nights broken by a passion of musical fits and seizures.

Aleck releases notes from his body. Until Signor Bertini claps his hands together and the piano stops singing. Aleck sits alone in his own silence.

When Aleck walks down to supper, he can't hear the grandfather clock in the hall, his mother's hands slapping against dough, his bare feet slapping wood. This temporary ear popping, the vengeful defiance of his body. Testing. Deaf like his mother but defiant. Aleck's ears shut out even the memory of sound. He can't imagine what her lip formations expect. Aleck can't hear her speak. She raises her ear-horn so Aleck will pour words into its mouth.

His lips form the words: Good evening, Mother. His tongue complies, *bon appétit*. Sound slithers out of his mouth.

Against the will of his body that commands silence. Demands silence.

Aleck's body refuses to let him hear, yet here he is, faking speech. His mother adjusts her ear-horn, curls her fingers from the direction of his mouth toward the inside of her hearing contraption. This motion pushes air between their faces. She indicates he should repeat his words. Good evening, Mother, his lips perform sound perfectly, she doesn't guess at the lack inside his ears. Neither son nor mother hears the words, but their struggle reverberates against both pairs of ears.

All week Aleck swims in the absence of noise. All week he refuses to approach his piano. For a week, he sleeps without moaning. The silence a seduction. When his father's lips flap at him, he turns away. Signor Bertini despairs. Aleck's father despairs. But his mother waits. This deafness the opposite of his frenzied seizures. Eliza knows Aleck is composed of extremes. She waits for him to swing again toward sound.

SUMMERS WITH GRANDFATHER mean afternoon walks to increase the appetite and lunches that begin in the morning. Aleck and Grandfather speak the same language; both belong in another city, both require the company of machines. Together they visit every ridiculous exhibit, every circus. They dare each other to catch out frauds. What they love best are machines they can hear. Bits of metal and string coaxed into speech by some inventor with more time than brains.

A duck that quacks and flaps its wings: Quaint. The wings don't bend but fold together like praying hands.

Flying and singing birds: Commonplace. Probably constructed by clockmakers in Switzerland. The notes are too sweet, too high to radiate.

A tambourine player: The figure sways in time to its music. Both Alexanders think him splendid.

Vaucanson's flute player: He barely looks human, but Aleck and his grandfather admit that the notes are accurate enough.

An automaton named Psycho: Reputed to be a ferocious whist player. Ho hum.

Chess players: *These* are a real mystery. The figures wear iron gloves yet manage to move the delicate wooden pieces flawlessly. The crowd yells for one or the other to move his King's Bishop's Pawn or Queen's Rook. Occasionally, the figures halt, midmove, and place a carved chess piece where the crowd advises. Aleck watches a challenger from the crowd lose his cash and his dignity. They must be hearing machines. They must be listening. There's no room in these metal men for human beings. Yet they can hear. And play chess like experts. They can hear, but they can't manage the simulation of speech.

The chess automatons never tire, never stop.

GRANDFATHER TAKES Aleck to view the Baron von Kempelen's automaton. They've never heard one talk before. The Baron has been dead for years and years, so chronologically, his automaton predates the others. There it sits, just like the others, beeping and gurgling and even burping once. How is this possible? Aleck asks. Grandfather reads the book and verifies the mathematics. He explains certain passages to Aleck. Here, Grandfather says, pointing out a figure of two men seated facing each other across a wall of wires and electronic connections. And here, he points to the laborious writing. The tones childish, but almost natural. In Grandfather's library, Aleck sits for hours, deciphering Kempelen's *Mécaniques de parole des Hommes*. Why would a German baron write in French? A book full of diagrams and drawings of a device that knows how to animate itself. A book full of typed words and marks on a page that mean an invention. Aleck displays himself in Grandfather's library. How clever he is, Grandfather's friends remark when they observe him there, how dedicated. A book full of ordinary math that, all put together, makes a metal contraption recite the King's English. How is this possible? Aleck asks himself. And if one such machine can be constructed, why not another? Why not another?

ALECK OPENS a museum. He collects the leg bones of squirrels and mice, the tailbone of a cat, labels each in Latin. He finds an entire sparrow skeleton, dusty and disintegrating, and figures out that birds fly because their bones are hollow. He thought flight was about feathers and wings. He has discovered a trick, then, one of Melly's gimmicks. He feels cheated of his admiration for flying creatures.

Aleck learns how to preserve plants and insects in his mother's leftover jars with cheesecloth tied around the tops. Aleck's ambition: to be a scientist, a collector of facts. Melly stares at the dragonflies, praying mantis, bluebottles Aleck has collected, but loses interest when Aleck reads droning lists of species and genera. Aleck knows more than Melly. He has discovered from the inside how a ladybird works. Next, he will tackle the touch of a finger against a cat's tongue, the echo of ocean caught inside a spiral shell.

2

Thought Book of A. Graham Bell

TODAY, MELLY AND I MADE A MACHINE SPEAK WORDS. We worked all this past month. Melly hauled spare wood from the lumber mill, armload by armload of discarded planks the owner let us drag away. Melly's arms are scraped red from loose nails from splinters. I sneaked into Mother's piano room and removed a long thin tube, perfect for magnifying sound, from her hearing apparatus.

I shaped replicas of the jaws, teeth and nasal cavities. Melly did the throat. I stretched gutta-percha rubber over the leftover planks Melly cut. Then padded the rubber with cotton to soften the air passages.

I thought of that after sticking my finger down my own throat. I want the creature's insides to feel real.

A machine that talks like the Baron's. It doesn't look like much, but we made it cry and call out and speak the word *Mama*.

Mama, Mama, it cried all morning long. The neighbors thought it was a real baby and asked why we didn't do something about the poor child! Ha. I knew it would work. Melly wanted to spend more time on the lips and belly, but I knew it would work.

Melly has soft hands like Mother's, his whole personality there. The rhythm of him scraping rough brick against wood sang to me: Melly can fix it, Melly can fix it.

The Baron's book wasn't enough. The diagrams are charcoal shadings of the human skull. We needed to know how the *inside* worked. That's what I kept explaining to Melly, that we needed to know, that we couldn't construct a proper larynx without dissecting one for real.

We have to make the sacrifice, I told him. Our cat in exchange for knowledge. Science beats out the cat every time, I told him. She lay so quiet in my hands. She trusted my hands. While I poured the nitric acid down her throat, I shut my eyes so I wouldn't hear the scream, but Melly said the acid burnt away her vocal cords too fast for there to be a scream. I hadn't thought the acid would destroy her vocal cords completely. Now she's useless.

Her head disintegrated. The hole in her throat grew and swallowed her jaw and cheeks and ears. Then the skin and fur over her skull disappeared into her eye sockets. But so slowly.

Melly managed to keep his eyes open the whole time?!

We had to use a lamb after that. And kill it without wrecking vital body parts. Melly slit its throat in one stroke. Except for the gash, the insides were intact.

When we finished we blew our breath into its lungs, and that's how the thing breathes. Breathes and talks, which means it's almost human. *Ah*, it said when we first opened up the diaphragm. A word, first thing! And all by itself.

Last year I made our dog bark out labial syllables:

*mmmmm*s and *bbbbb*s, and this year a mechanical thing
that pronounces an actual word. I can make anything
speak. A coatrack maybe. Pebbles. The clock in the hall.
Balloons. Melly's favorite top hat. Melly pulls ridiculous
objects out of it, and all the uncles and cousins adore
him. But I'll make magic tricks look tame beside speech.
What would my shoes say if I asked them to report on
the quality of the cobblestone today? Or my elbows about
how thin my sweater has become? I know, I'll talk to
Father's pipe and ask it to repeat entire after-dinner conversations.

Melly doesn't even care about the prize Father offered
for inventing speech, but I'm going to ask for a real
human skull.

3

Edinburgh Grows Small for Aleck

ALECK'S FATHER INVENTS SPEECH.

Mr. Bell listens to Aleck recite his *Hamlet* soliloquy and transcribes the whole thing into pages and pages of loops and twirls. He hears Aleck and Melly argue—My turn now, my turn—and writes that down, too. He listens to a woodpecker outside the window and tries to make the same noises out of pen and ink. Aleck is so bored he wants to scream at his father. When he does his father writes that down, too.

Aleck stands up and rushes to his father's writing table. He can't believe his father has been so busy listening that he has lost the knack of hearing. There it is on paper: Aleck's scream.

Can you read it back to me? Aleck demands, and rests his hand on his father's shoulder so Mr. Bell will answer the question, not just transcribe it.

Aleck's father whirls, stares at his son, wondering at the touch. Aleck has ignored his father's work for so long.

Mr. Bell picks up the paper and blows on the ink till it dries. Softly, he clears his throat and gently coughs.

Then lets an ear-rupturing scream out of his mouth.

Father and son stare at one another in disbelief. Then both break down laughing, more and more until Aleck hurts, until he tries to stop but can't. In the midst of this laughing, his father writes down their laughter, too, writes down laughing at writing down laughing.

And not just their laughter, but the strange animal noises of Aleck trying to stop.

ALECK'S FATHER invents speech.

Words don't look on the page the way they should. He divides the alphabet into vowels and consonants. He divides the mouth into regions and makes a map of it. His system is a phonetics for linguists to decipher. Look at that squiggle and make this noise, he instructs Aleck. Aleck can make any noise he sees. Aleck is the ideal pupil for his father's paper-thin invention.

Aleck sits in his father's study and watches his father invent a way of writing that looks like horseshoes and whips.

Mr. Bell's sons perform for public audiences.

Aleck's father draws ^ on a blackboard, and it means a sound. I can make my son say this sound, he tells his gathered audience. Say ^ Aleck, say ^ . Aleck does. ^ says Aleck, ^ ^ ^ .

Then his father draws more lines and dots on the blackboard. His first public demonstration on word pronunciation. He turns to the men: A test, he says to the bearded faces.

Out of the room goes Aleck. Melly remains behind. Aleck's face shines as he walks, slowly, past the grunting mumbling academics.

Offer me words, Mr. Bell demands from his audience. Difficult words. Nonsense. Words from a language you don't even believe in.

Sszeckeeeh SHAY AY, shouts one voice. Outside the double-wooded door, Aleck doesn't hear, can't even imagine the sounds these men will invent for him.

Yes. Again, says Mr. Bell. More.

Pfu ZUM blah, goes the audience, *w?xim^blu*.

Mr. Bell makes the blackboard into art. Draws alphabets with strokes and gashes through the characters. Dots and wavy lines above that. The blackboard, propped on a podium, faces the audience. Aleck outside. Not hearing.

Watch, says Mr. Bell. You'll see. He brings in Aleck, who studies the board, studies the silent anticipating audience. No muttering now. Melly lost beside their father. Melly, the oldest, but Aleck holds the audience inside his voice, carries the scribbles on the blackboard from his throat out over the tops of men's heads.

Sszeckeeeh SHAY AY, repeats Aleck. Looks at his father. *Pfu ZUM blah*, he quotes, *wʔximˆblu.*

ALECK NEVER tells Grandfather he inserted another name between the two they both owned. At fourteen, he memorizes the soliloquies of Hamlet in Grandfather's study. At fifteen, Grandfather divides the summer between Latin and Greek. Aleck seeks an escape that is more than just summers. He applies to boys' schools for the position of piano instructor. Instead—because of his father's name and reputation—the school at Elgin offers him the position of elocution tutor. He'll be a teacher then.

Grandfather taught the British how to speak English. Aleck's father invents on paper a vision of how to hear. Aleck will do both. There are no automatons at Elgin, but his days will be filled with an imagination that begins in the lungs.

Sixteen, Aleck departs his father's house and steps into a future he can only taste.

ALECK LOOKS out of his bedroom window and sees people marching in the direction of elsewhere. Aleck slips down the back stairs and out into the garden. His mother needs him to interpret her world through his fingers. There she is: Eliza, half blinded by the sun's halo, easel propped against the landscape. How delicate her fingers, Aleck thinks. Eliza famous all over Edinburgh for her miniature paintings, her replicas of local bankers and mayors. Aleck observes her interpretation of their garden pulpit, blades of grass. She will never be a great landscape artist.

Aleck matches his own profile with his mother's and approaches her in a straight line. She cannot hear his footsteps. She will not notice his shadow reaching her painting easel. Her chin lifts toward the blue above her head, and she strokes yellowed skylines onto her canvas. Blue, yellow. Blue, yellow. Eliza's fingers dip into the canvas, stroke old paint. Her fingers avoid the fresh oil she has added today. The sun is too bright. Aleck closes his eyes then realizes his mother has done the same. Deaf by nature, blind by choice, his mother confronts a canvas of sound. She strokes her fingers into the branches she has carved, as Aleck's fingers stroke piano keys. She hears the scritch of birch. Aleck has no talent for painting. Eliza tilts her left ear to catch a ripple of leaves rearranging themselves. Aleck will never translate the words her skin hears.

On Sunday Aleck accompanies his mother to church. He fingerspells the preacher's darting words. Sixteen and bored, Aleck cradles both hands in his mother's lap and twists his knuckles around a lesson from the Bible. Mr. Bell refuses Anglicanism. Melly has recently embraced Spiritualism. Nobody can spell as fast as Aleck. Melly's fingers are thick, like their mother's, too set in their ways. Aleck's fingers crawl the air before his mind knows what his hands will say. His mother divides her face between Aleck's hands in her lap and the preacher's face. The two combined make a sermon.

Aleck no longer displays interest in the game of translation but finds himself still seated in the half dark, listening to an old man promise platonic love to old women. If he could think that fast, Aleck would command his fingers to convey a different message, superimpose his own interpretation on the preacher's words. But his fingers are too quick for him, and they spell out several sentences before his mind registers hearing a sound. Aleck is defeated by his own abilities. Amen, he spells to his mother. Amen, she says out loud.

Since trading in God for the lesser known qualities of the supernatural, Melly's skills and talent for magic have doubled. He used to pass ribbons through his mother's wedding band, and the ribbons changed colors. Parlor tricks in the evening. But Melly starts to believe in his own talent for astonishing. An ordinary kitchen chair folds into kindling, then shapes itself back into a chair. Melly smashes their grandfather's favorite timepiece, and Aleck fears the beating that will follow. Grandfather explodes into laughter. He, too, has come to believe in the watch's reincarnation. Believes Melly can revive anything.

Melly reads minds. He requests a volunteer. Aleck cowers behind chairs, but Melly has lost interest in his younger sibling and chooses a woman Aleck hadn't even noticed enough to ignore. Green beans, Melly reads from his list. Striped trousers, antlers, ants-in-your-pants. Caroline blushes at Aleck's brother's precision. Your sister's yellow hairpin, an envelope full of stamps from another country, green eyes. Melly discovers sugar candies in Caroline's hair. She accepts his hand when he offers to make her disappear.

SIXTEEN, Aleck stops fingerspelling to his mother. The exercise reminds him of Melly's oh-so-clever parlor tricks. It galls him that his mother cannot hear his voice except through the machinery of her hearing tube. He wants his voice inside her ears. Look at me, listen to me, Aleck pleads. But he only says this out loud, only speaks into the air. His words never reach his mother.

The hearing tube becomes the enemy. Aleck refuses speech into a machine. You can hear me if you try, he says to his mother, says to her eyes. She remembers the sounds lips make, but cannot fathom the sight of them. Her son's lips exclude her. Aleck expects her eyes to do the work of now useless ears. Except they're not useless, not when she can insert her magnifying tube into an eardrum. But Aleck won't be satisfied with props.

Aleck touches his mouth against her ear and shouts himself hoarse. The noise is too big, she tells him, and blurry. Aleck doesn't give up. He shouts his voice at her from different points in a room. Can you hear me now? Can you hear me now? His mother shakes her head at his lips. He tries closer, he tries tilting his head backward. He makes her angle her neck until the ground sways. He walks a straight line toward her mouth. He cups both hands against her ears. He tries talking into the skin wrapped around her throat. He keeps shouting into her ears, can you hear me now? Eliza hears less and less every day. She stares at her son's lips. Furiously. Can you hear me now? his question always the same. Of course she can hear him, just not his words. Yes, she tells him when his lips crush against her left temple. I can hear you Aleck. I can hear.

4

Aleck and Melly Play Who am I?

ALECK AND MELLY SIT ON THE FLOOR IN THE PARLOR. Melly goes first because he is the oldest. The two brothers sit cross-legged, solemn. Melly, the oldest, the one carrying his father's name, the innovator, the scholar. Aleck, two years behind, dreamer, artist, child.

They hold hands. Melly pulls Aleck forward. Melly's hands the bigger, the stronger. Melly pulls Aleck inside the circle that is their arms. Their cat rubs Aleck's leg; their arms keep her out.

Guess my secret, Melly says. Their arms wrapped around each other's arms, their heads together. Aleck, his foot asleep, thinks: the blood can't get in. Thinks: I can't move. Says: Give me a hint. Melly watches his younger brother rock forward onto his knees. Thinks: Aleck has no patience. Thinks: Aleck is too eager. Aleck rocks ankle-to-knee; his fingers grip Melly's. Melly, patient and strong. Aleck, weaker.

I am, Melly chants, a thing so vast, no mortal being has ever seen me. Aleck pulls away; Melly holds fast. No fair being God, says Aleck. Melly smiles. You're so dumb, he says. You're so dumb. Aleck closes his eyes. Who is Melly if he can't see him? The sky? No, *dummy*. Heaven? No.

Aleck squeezes his eyes tighter, thinks about Melly's hands, his fingers squeezing, his fingers squeezed. Aleck opens his eyes, stares at his brother's hands.

Not strong at all, he thinks. I could overpower those hands, he thinks. They're Mother's hands. On the sofa, the cat stretches; her paws reach above her head. The bottom of the ocean, Aleck says. Smiles Melly's smile. Melly lets go, shakes his hands free, gets up. But it's my turn now, Aleck says. It's my turn.

AFTER GRANDFATHER'S DEATH, the family moves into his home in London. Aleck wants nothing more than to stay behind in Edinburgh. Melly, the oldest son, gets to stay behind to represent them all. Aleck can't stand the house in Harrington Square without his grandfather. His father doesn't know how to carry off opulence. Aleck's father scoffs at the Eton jacket, kid gloves and ebony cane Aleck hauls out of the hall closet. The clothes still fit, and Aleck insists on wearing them to stroll out in the public gardens. He prowls the streets of London alone: no Grandfather, no Melly.

Without Grandfather's rigorous monitoring of his time, Aleck has no deadlines. Summer in London has become sticky and slow, and Aleck is not used to slow. In London, without Grandfather, Aleck drifts. He sits in the garden to compose letters to Melly but forgets to bring Grandfather's fountain pen. He offers to run errands for his mother, then forgets where he's headed. Every day, morning becomes afternoon. Aleck longs for school and discipline. Next year at Elgin, he will schedule every minute, make his boys follow the rules.

MELLY MAILS a thick packet to the family from Edinburgh filled with fabulous Melly tricks:

Bits and pieces of grout and mortar Melly has scraped from the house where they used to live.

The front page of a newspaper.

A transparent scarf that manages to be a different color on each side.

A rolled-up canvas their mother painted before she married, which Melly discovered in an antique store.

A child's glove.

A papier–mâché map of Scotland with only the rivers painted in and the name *Caroline, Caroline, Caroline* written in black ink all over the surface of the land.

A handwritten page in Visible Speech, for his father, of Xhosa clicks Melly learned from a seafaring native of Natal.

A ten-page letter for his mother.

And half a sheet of instructions for Aleck:

Don't lie down on heated ground

Don't crawl into caves

Don't psalmsing in a choir

Don't mix pickles with beer

Don't neglect the English language or geometry

Don't fail to rank music in your lists

Don't hate London—for home's sake

Don't doubt the constant affection of Father

Don't doubt

MELLY'S LETTERS from Edinburgh grow more numerous by the month. Everything Aleck knows about Melly now he learns from the inside of an envelope. Melly's engagement, the stammering students he tutors. Even Melly's tricks continue. Melly sends Aleck a newspaper article about the Great Loblinski appearing at the Edinburgh Music Hall. Aleck understands from this coded announcement that audiences are seduced and beguiled by his brother, the bearded Russian Prestidigitator.

And then Melly gets sick. Tuberculosis. The letters turn into scrawled half-notes and jagged thoughts until Aleck receives only one sentence at a time or just an envelope filled with scraps of paper that used to be for Melly's words.

I'm coughing my life away, Melly writes. Every thought I've ever consumed trumpets violently from my body. I am afraid to inhale, for who knows what I will breathe back out?

Melly sends Aleck another long list of instructions titled: How to Communicate with the Dead. Melly's handwriting is so bad by now, Aleck thinks he wrote Communication with the *Deaf*, and puzzles over the chants and candles Melly insists are vital to the process.

CURES FOR TUBERCULOSIS:

cod liver oil
raw eggs in wine
breathe a pure atmosphere
wear flannel against your skin
walk
mixture of: hops, spikenard root, inner & outer
    portions of tamarack bark boiled together,
    drained, drink quick with honey & brandy

IF ANYONE CAN get out of this, Melly can. Wave your magician's wand, Melly. Bend the coffin backward till it forms the letter *C*.

Melly in a box. Aleck stares at the face that isn't a face, at the hands that aren't hands. Aleck expects Melly to rise out of the coffin, declare the whole thing a joke, a trick, laugh and exclaim: Who am I? and then cough and cough and cough until blood pours out his nostrils.

Don't lie there, Melly. Open your mouth, pull pin-cushions out of your fingertips, suck on lollipops and rocks from our garden. Sit up, Melly. Wave at me. C'mon, Melly, wave your magician's wand.

Melly lying there. One finger crooked over his chest, accidentally pointing at his chin. Everything about Melly is accidental now. Aleck stands quietly in his pew, watch-es aunts, uncles, neighbors, friends of Melly he's never met gather to kiss his dead brother's dead cheek. Aleck whispers: I know you, he says to the inert body. I know you. You're thinking you're no longer alive, and you don't have to say anything anymore. Well, you're wrong.

Aleck wants to caress Melly's cheek, to lean down for a kiss of life.

I've only got one chance, Melly, Aleck speaks into the coffin. Who am I? But Melly is stone cold silent, and all Aleck can do is repeat: Who am I? His fingers, scrunched against Melly's coffin, spell out this final question.

LAST ONE HOME'S a rotten egg, Melly yells over his shoulder, daring Aleck to push past, daring Aleck to be first.

And Aleck runs hardest fastest, scissors his legs to chase Melly round and round the marble pulpit in their garden in Edinburgh. Not once did he ever succeed in getting close. Melly knows which way to turn to cut the corner closest so his heels dig into the dirt and how to torque his body to the left, to the right, so Aleck skids to the ground in poor imitation.

Melly runs and never looks back.

But Melly is in a box in the ground. Aleck is closer to being ahead than ever before in his life. Aleck, twenty-three and advancing; Melly, stopped at twenty-five. In two years, Aleck will pass his older brother.

The trick to being first, Aleck learned from the funeral, is allowing yourself to be last.

THEY BURY Melly beside Grandfather Bell. What's awful is that Melly is in a hole in the ground, and Aleck's father already believes Aleck next in line. Mr. Bell decides, on account of Aleck's too-predictable coughing, to ensure this son's survival. Aleck's coughing mimics Melly's. Mr. Bell decides to transport his family to a safe place, to a new country free from dust and grime. Aleck discovers his father expects him to leave Britain simply because he is still alive. He refuses. He isn't sensible; he isn't reasonable. He wants to remain behind. To take his father's phonetic alphabet, his father's Visible Speech charts, his father's reputation, and do more with them than his father ever could. Not just imitate his father's sounds but create new ones.

But in order to be from a place, you must leave that place. Aleck is going to be from Edinburgh, from London, from Canada. Homes he learns to leave behind; countries he no longer belongs to.

LAST ONE HOME gets to close the door. Or leave it open for others to follow. Aleck, recovering from illness, will lie dying in Canada. It will not be enough for him to translate unwritten Indian languages into his father's Visible Speech. Not interested in the process of visualizing articulation, Aleck wants to create sound out of sound.

From here, there will be two possibilities: Aleck will invent the telephone; Aleck won't invent the telephone. Aleck doesn't know which way he'll go. The telephone, he knows, has already been invented. But not for the last time.

Aleck won't leave any doors open, not even a crack. He'll have to make sure, though, that he is inside before this door slams shut for good.

5

Letters from Marie

AT ELGIN, ALECK TEACHES BOYS PROPER SPEECH. They can tell him anything so long as they use correct grammar, precise words, exact pronunciation. He expects the boys to ask him for his opinion on politics, for advice on how to control natural desires. The first boy complains that the soup wasn't hot enough, that he likes it piping. Yeah, says another, usually my mom sends biscuits, but she's broken her leg and I have to survive on what they serve us here. Aleck points to each one in turn. Tell me your name, he demands, and follow that with a complete sentence. Jeremy, announces a third boy. My big sister will visit this weekend. Marie once took the train all the way up the coast just to fetch a pair of socks. Not even white, neither. Either, says Aleck. Jeremy continues. She's stubborn and bossy. Girls don't know how to talk sense; their words go all over the place. Marie can talk a blue streak. Her words come out with no break; she must inhale through her ears. But Jeremy doesn't stop there: I warn you, he tells the other boys, tells Aleck, Marie doesn't slow down, never. Ever, says Aleck. Marie never gets silent, insists Jeremy, but she'll have goodies. Hang around and I promise, we'll get ripe lemons and custard tarts and melon cut into cubes. That's the thing; we'll get eats out of this visit. At least we'll get that.

MARIE CARRIES a large basket of fruit. No, she says to Jeremy's reaching hand, your new tutor shall have first pick. Marie is too tall and too confident. Aleck stares at her. Marie's limbs don't fit her body. She holds the basket with purple gloves that envelop her arms past her elbows. Aleck lowers his own arm into her offering, gathers a handful of grapes into his palm. Ripe grapes. In the middle of dreary November. Aleck holds them in his palm before popping one grape into his waiting mouth. His hands don't want to let go the cool reminders of spring. His tongue makes the shape of a grape inside his mouth. In Spain they peel them, Marie tells Aleck. A peeled grape is sun and eating meals outside. But I'm much too impatient. And you need the right clothes for that sort of thing. Clothing? What do clothes have to do with eating in Spain? Peeled grapes are the ultimate in patience and decadence, depending on which side of the peeling you're on, Marie continues. Peeled grapes disintegrate in your mouth without you having to chew. But you'll have to settle for these, she tells Jeremy and the others. I was too busy singing on the train. Aleck can't fathom how singing might prevent this girl from whittling grapes in her lap. Besides, Marie continues, I like the way grape skins feel slippery against your teeth, don't you? My teeth? Aleck wonders, chewing carefully.

SHOW ME your room, Marie insists to Jeremy. Take me on a tour of the school grounds. Jeremy doesn't want to walk her anywhere. Stay here, he says to his big sister. Sit awhile. Marie laughs and delivers her hug. She strolls out the door. The others follow. She carries an umbrella even though no one expects rain. Marie swings the umbrella round and round her shoulders without once letting the tip of it scratch the ground. Still, Aleck notices a flaw: Marie's umbrella is just a cover for a defective leg.

Marie's brother Jeremy is fifteen. Aleck himself is only sixteen, but none of the boys know this. Marie visits again before the end of term, each time letting Aleck choose first from her basket. He pulls out a pomegranate the second visit, and Marie tells the story of Persephone in hell. Persephone was so young, you see, she explains to Jeremy, explains to Aleck, she didn't know she'd be dragged underground forever. She didn't even know what forever meant; that's how young she was. In Marie's version, Persephone's mother transforms the soil, makes dust out of fertilized land. Persephone's mother invented winter, you see, Marie explains. Nobody had ever heard of seasons before, so they didn't know how to go about growing and then not growing. Seasons are about waiting. Persephone's mother waited, but Hades didn't know how. Men don't understand that having seasons can change everything.

MARIE REPLACES the fruit with chocolate. My sweet tooth, she tells Aleck, who has assigned written exercises for the first time this term. They still have classes, he tells her. We can save the chocolate for later. Oh no, Marie sucks the tip of one finger, I'll never last that long with chocolate dangling under my nose. Someday I'll have to escape to Germany because there they make the sexiest chocolate. Aleck blushes. He doesn't know how to reply to Marie's words.

The boys swarm the classroom as soon as they hear Marie's umbrella swishing air. She pushes them back. To let Aleck reach in first. Marie's dresses hide imbalance. Aleck has already guessed her handicap. He observes the way she carries one leg higher than the other. Marie carries stories in her head and laughs when she speaks them. I know you, she once said to Aleck. No, that must have been somebody else. Marie offers Aleck the heaping basket. Aleck declines, preferring whatever is left over. Go ahead boys, he gives them permission, take whatever you want. Aleck wants to recite lists of exotic fruit into Marie's ear: kumquat, coconut, starfruit. He wants to make her laugh *after* he reaches the end of a joke. He wants her to listen while he says her name, wants her to hear his voice whispering. By the time each boy has grabbed his succulent treasure, the basket is empty. But Aleck doesn't mind; Marie's empty basket holds more promise than when full.

ALECK WANTS one more good-bye. He rushes to the station, hoping to catch Marie before her train departs. But there stands Jeremy, dawdling, tugging at Marie's umbrella spokes, not leaving his sister alone. Marie laughs and steps onto one of the carriages, leans out to throw fabulous words at her younger brother's waiting ears: rhinoceros, pimpernel, horticulture, able-bodied.

Frustrated, Aleck pulls out his pad and draws Marie's face. Sketches the shadows behind her ears and chin. Marie is not quite complete when the train begins to pull away.

That night Aleck writes in his diary, "I have become a victim of the excesses of love."

He hangs this picture above his bed. Marie's blurred mouth: what Aleck stares at before falling asleep.

IN THE SCHOOL visiting garden, Aleck recites to Marie the names of the men who precede him: Nasmyth invented the steam hammer. Fairbairn, the iron steamship. Marie stares at a cucumber plant that shouldn't be grown beside flowers. Cucumbers need more light, she says, and mounds and mounds more earth. MacMillan, the mechanical simplicity of pedal bicycles. Marie leans down to urge the blooms to burst into seed. Come on, she says to the cucumber stalk, come on. Bells.

During Aleck's monologue, Marie stares one by one at the pistils and stems of the daisies decorating the path. These daisies have no conversation, yet Marie pays more attention to them than to her brother's tutor. She daydreams a magic trick perhaps or some hocus-pocus like Melly might perform. Aleck's voice increases its monotonous rhythm: Edinburgh men, Marie, that's where I come from. He sits under the weak sun and recites heroes. He ignores Marie's ignoring.

Melly, too, flutters his ears past Aleck's words, invents a new trick while Aleck's voice demands a portion of his brother's ear. Or Melly holds Caroline's hand, the two of them pretending to listen, the two of them shutting him out. This is the way of older and younger brothers. Of lovers.

In a combination of three, one is always left out.

The difference in the equation now is that there is no third person, only Marie and Aleck. And Aleck's conviction that he must recapture her ears. Marie pays no attention to Aleck's heroic narrative. Her gaze shifts to her lap, through the grass, across Aleck's ankles.

Stop staring, Aleck protests, after Marie has spent a full five minutes peering at the soles of his feet. What are you looking for?

Marie points an orange-gloved finger to where Aleck, in a moment of abandon, has exposed his skin. I can find letters between your toes, she says. There's a *V* and *T* and *M* and *W* and even an *X* etched into the soles of your feet. Neat, huh? she smiles at the bellies of his toes.

Aleck never allows his boys slang. You're not listening to me, he grumbles at her. Listen to me, Marie. Don't stare at what doesn't matter. Aleck rolls over until his face is upside down beneath Marie's eyes. There, he says, speaking into her forehead. Stare at that.

Okay. Marie complies, stares hard at the tip of Aleck's nose. He begins to notice that her eyes are not focused on his own. Damn! he wishes to shout, but will not in front of a girl. Instead he shoves his socks and Elgin shoes back onto his feet, walks away from Marie's haphazard staring. Oh Aleck, she calls after his back, I can see stories no matter where I look.

ALECK DIVES into teaching at Elgin. This year, he will study for the degree examinations at London University. He will teach by day, study by night. Weekends for Marie.

Except: Marie's brother has disappeared. None of Aleck's students know why he has not returned or where he might have gone. Some seem not to remember Jeremy, not even when Aleck mentions the baskets of fruit. The white and green parasol. Aleck returned to Elgin because of Marie. And now he can't find her.

Aleck invades the records office, searching the files for Jeremy or a last name he didn't know about or an old address he can trace. At night, he throws the blanket off his sweating body and composes letters to the sketch of her face above his bed. Mornings, he crumples the pages and hurls them into the river beneath his window. By noon, he is in the records office, prowling. The secretary has become used to Aleck rummaging among the stacks of old files and record boxes. Young and too poor to attend school at Elgin, the secretary works in the school's offices instead of at a mill with his father. He watches Aleck's spine as he reaches down into yet another crate stuffed full of yellowed papers. The secretary has to stop himself from bumping his fingers along that curved spine. He doesn't care if Aleck ever catches up with whatever he's pursuing.

WHEN THE LETTER ARRIVES from Marie, Aleck feels ridiculous. Of course she writes him letters. Of course she is planning a visit next weekend. She will be at the train station at 10:00 A.M.

Aleck is at the station at 8:57. In his arms, a picnic basket heaped with cucumber sandwiches and biscuits and water from the spring. Everything he could think of except fruit. He will take her for a short walk along the river, and just before they come to the cliffs, they will picnic. Aleck plans the day in his head: pick up Marie, short walk, lunch, return to the school's grounds, a short talk about his future, the good-bye kiss. He checks the station clock again. Only ten minutes have passed. He plans the day again, this time putting in more details: the ridge overlooking a bend in the river where there's a broken tree trunk Marie can rest on. He'll ask her about Jeremy, then where she goes to school. He'll sneak looks at her face though she won't notice. He'll point to clouds that form giraffes or elephants, then look at her looking.

The station clock must be slow. Aleck fills in more and more details: a freckle just below Marie's left nostril, how her left skirt drags the ground though she pretends not to care, how strong her arms are; she swings them high over her head when she talks; her gloves color the sky purple, green, orange; she waves her arms in any direction except down. Perhaps she thinks she can propel herself forward with her arms, Aleck thinks. Perhaps her arms help her walk.

When Marie steps off the train onto the platform, Aleck's legs are already tired from walking round and round the same path, his throat sore from rehearsing his dialogue.

MARIE, limping and huffing, refuses to stop until they reach Aleck's first lookout. The morning's only half used up, but Marie prefers to keep going.

But we have to stop, Aleck argues. The cliffs make the path too steep after this.

Maybe for you, Marie throws over her shoulder, but I want to see more. Aleck, lagging behind in an effort to slow Marie down, hasn't yet had the chance to study Marie's face. It grates on his ears when she throws words over her shoulder. Throws words away.

Okay, he says, okay. We'll walk to the cliffs. He stops himself just before the words—I'll take you—escape his mouth. Marie won't like that at all. Already Aleck knows this.

Let's go in, Marie says when they reach a cave that reveals itself only after they have climbed folds of hill that crunch dirt into tough layers of higher climbing. The walk was a bad idea, Aleck admits to himself. Marie's bad leg isn't strong enough even if she digs her umbrella deep into the rust-colored soil. But Marie doesn't think so. She turns and points her chin at him, her lips just beginning to part: A cave! A cave, Aleck! Perhaps he should argue. Perhaps he should insist they return.

Marie carries her dainty umbrella in one hand and pine cones in the other. She leans slightly to the right for balance. Her limp is more noticeable now that she has roots and fallen branches to negotiate. The path angles steeply, and Aleck pictures Marie falling many times before she actually does. Aleck struggles behind to where Marie lies in the dirt, his head filled with what awful hurt her face might express. Aleck's eyes focus instead on the awkward rhythm of her shoulders vibrating through laughter. By the time he is ready to face her face, Marie is ready to jump up again, limp forward, yell back in his direction.

Colander, she says, my mother always throws a bit into the soup. Edelweiss; tastes best with cheese and crackers. Boxed bruises; Father once won a prize for growing them. Happenstance; I've never seen any this close to a river. Corkbread; Jeremy used to braid that into my hair.

Aleck grunts in reply. His voice creaks when he tries to answer Marie. And when she does, finally, turn her head toward him, Aleck can see her lips are full of laughter, her eyes know how much he doesn't know.

Marie crawls on her hands and knees inside the cave, her gloved hands grabbing at rocks. Aleck follows her cautiously and upright. His shoulders scrape the jagged ceiling. They sit with their backs toward the opening and stare at the contracting walls that disappear into night. They have retreated so far that the cave opening is only a mouth, a tiny puff of whistle that neither can hear. Marie opens the basket and pulls out Aleck's soggy lunch. What, no fruit? she asks, but he doesn't need to see her face to recognize the smile. I'll bet these caves are full of bats, Marie declares. I'll bet all the silence we hear is them screaming at the stalactites, trying to detect where we are. That's ridiculous, Aleck replies. He can't exactly offer her comfort. She is not hinting for support or for his arm around her shoulder. But he can't figure why Marie yanks him out of his regular life, drags him halfway up a bloody mountain, then yammers on about bats. This is what he must decipher: how to crack Marie's code of speaking, translate it into a language he can recognize.

If he sits quietly, he will manage to calm Marie. She

needs rest after that ridiculous hike. Aleck closes his eyes, expecting to feel delicately gloved fingers press against his lids. Instead, Marie's words tickle his ears:

Are you always so morose? she asks. Her voice comes to him from way down near the entrance. He hasn't even heard her move. Gradually, his eyes fighting the dark, he makes out her silhouette and one hand rubbing the muscles of her left leg.

THEY GET BACK to Elgin around dusk. Marie's dress, white and yellow when she stepped off the train, appears brown and reddish. Aleck dreads letting her back on the train looking so disheveled, but there is nowhere at the school for girls to wash or change. Her shoddiness appears less temporary than Aleck's dusty trousers. And her expression refuses to acknowledge shame.

Marie swings her parasol into the air and catches it with one hand. The parasol is bent and torn from Marie bracing her weight against it on the way down. She opens it anyway and shows Aleck the sky through the holes. Like we're back in the cave again, she says, except with so many more exits and entrances.

Aleck rushes her along to the train station so she can at least wash the bottom of her dress, which is weighed down with caked reddish mud. Silly, she laughs, it's much easier to get off once it's dry. Not at all like blood, you know. Once a month I have to rush straight from my bed to the bathroom and scrub and scrub and scrub with water cold enough to freeze pimples off your back.

Aleck stops walking and faces the train. Marie kisses him on the tip of his nose and proceeds, humming a tune Aleck can't quite catch. Marie doesn't realize Aleck has no sisters. He's never heard a woman speak about her body. Except his mother about her useless ears and disintegrating hearing. Even mentioning a bathroom seems so unladylike he can hardly stand there long enough to wave good-bye. What an unpleasantly talkative girl, Aleck decides. Whatever was I thinking? Marie jumps onto the first step and swings the damaged parasol around in a circle. Look, she calls out to Aleck, I'm a giant clock. I'm a propeller.

There are so many languages Aleck can't yet speak.

MARIE IS NOW in Germany, but she could get back in time, before Aleck's father's plan takes effect. If Aleck marries Marie, there'll be no more talk of leaving. Aleck spends days collecting the most exact and appropriate proposals. He reads Keats's love poems. Before she left for her holiday, Marie crammed herself full of German words, none of them for Aleck.

After Melly's funeral, Aleck expects to hear Marie's words pour into his ear, expects a written incarnation of love. He writes her an appeal. He writes to her and writes to her. Marie is his solution.

But Marie doesn't return to England. She announces her plans to study German physics in Taunus. Marie's letter promises futures he can't yet recognize: Make a name for yourself there, Aleck. Make a name for yourself in a country where Bell isn't a church ornament but whatever story you invent for yourself. Go forward, Aleck. Don't hang onto this place. Don't hang onto what no longer lives here.

Aleck has explained, using his grandfather's exacting grammar, that he misses her. In the margins of his luke-warm proposal of passion, he copies Latin quotes from Virgil and Catullus.

Marie ignores his marginalia. She writes back: How I shall miss you all! Funny, I don't expect you will return, England having become too *slow* for you.

So Aleck goes to America and becomes someone else.

BEFORE THEY LEAVE England, Aleck sells his brother's house, his brother's piano. The house was easy, but how can he leave Melly without a piano? Aleck sits at the keyboard and tries to play a hymn. No, a hymn's wrong for Melly. Aleck wonders if there's such a thing as a séance song. Maybe he can conjure Melly with mystical chants.

The notes won't follow his fingers. Aleck presses his foot against the pedal that lifts the felt dampers from the piano wires. Hums to himself. He bangs out Christmas Carols and Dickens' Follies. Melly lies dead but his piano stays tuned.

The notes reverberate insincerely around Melly's vacant house so Aleck stops playing, but his foot remains depressed. The piano sighs and Aleck hums along with its fading notes, hums along with the piano humming.

Melly's piano humming.

Aleck stops and the piano stops. He hums and the piano hums. Then he lifts the dampers carefully so the wires can't possibly be vibrating because of Aleck letting his foot go. Aleck leans down, sings into Melly's piano, pours his voice into the heart of Melly's instrument.

The piano wires sing back.

In perfect pitch.

Sympathetic vibrations. Melly's piano has learned how to sing by itself. Without Melly. Sympathy vibrations in response to Aleck's voice. Echoing out of the piano. A parlor trick. The kind Melly might have performed for friends had he discovered it himself. Aleck, alone with his own voice and Melly's piano. He hits middle C, works his way to each end and back. One note at a time. Again. Then hits middle C. Again. And again.

Aleck adores the clear clean music of a single note played over and over, his head thick as fog.

He closes the piano carefully and wipes it clean for the new owners.

6

The Thought Books of A. Graham Bell

FATHER TOOK US TO VISIT GRANDFATHER'S GRAVE TODAY. Five years he's been underground. Five years since I saw his face move beneath its skin. Melly smiled at the fresh flowers Father pays a custodian to plant every spring. Grandfather's not really down there, Melly said. He's walking around beside us during the day.

Last time I stayed with Grandfather, six years ago, I never told him, but I saw the Reis exhibit that toured London. Grandfather was busy with one of his old cronies, so I slipped out for a walk around Harrington Square. Except I walked and walked until I found that poster we'd passed the day before. Reis—Somebody— had invented a device that conveyed sound.

He named it his telephone.

The thing was ugly. He'd hollowed out a bung from a beer barrel, covered it with sausage skin and stuck on strips of platinum with bits of sealing wax. What a laugh, I thought. Wait'll Grandfather hears this one.

And then the crude thing *worked*. No strings attached. I heard the tinny notes of a harpsichord transmitted from another room. I heard the notes rise out of the *metal*, not through the wires. Nor through the walls. I couldn't very well relate that story to Grandfather. He once deduced that the chess automatons we saw contained hidden dwarfs. Whatever would he do with *this* contraption?

That was ten years ago, but I can still hear that harpsichord resounding its notes. Why didn't Reis consider the human voice? Or did he? This is my next project, what I'm going to do when I get to America: invent the telephone all over again.

JUNE 11TH, 1870. LONDON

MELLY'S FUNERAL was awful. I stood by Father and Mother and held Carrie's hand and the congregation sang righteous hymns about returning to the bosom. Crap. Throughout the sermon, I could feel Carrie's wedding ring pressing into my palm, and I thought what a useless bit of jewelry now. That was all I could think about holding my brother's widow's hand, that her ring was biting into my skin. And what sort of ring I would have given Marie. Grandfather's probably. Since Melly's boy is dead, too, Grandfather's ring goes to me next. Too bad Marie won't have it. That ring would suit her rainbow fingers. Thoughts that should have been spent on Melly.

JULY 3RD, 1870. LONDON

CARRIE, the raving mad widow, and I, the absurd left-over brother: yelling at Melly to appear, jump out of the box, wave his magic hands in the air. I didn't even let go of Carrie's hand while I waved mine about. I'm sure to the rest of the congregation we looked a right pair of idiots. I felt bad for her, after. Carrie said it made for a scene, but scenes prove we're alive. She said she thinks more about the baby than about Melly. Not because she doesn't miss them both, only that she doesn't feel that Melly's dying was her fault. They gave the baby four names, too many for an infant. Maybe it wasn't the number but the kind of names. Who would want to grow into an Ottoway? Naturally, I didn't voice this out loud.

JULY 22ND, 1870. THE S.S. NESTORIAN

CAPTAIN HAS PROMISED me first view of shore.
Besides the crew, that is. So I won't really be first at all.
But Father has told him I'm ill, halfway to the grave, so
this must be how sailors humor the dying. But I've decided instead to retire to my cabin when the time comes.
You can't really urge a dying man to leave his bunk, can
you? I'll be the last of this lot to step onto Canada, but I
bet my brother's life I'll be the first to leave. When the
ship pulled away from England, I thought we'd seen the
last of Europe, but we stopped in Spain and Portugal
before embracing the open sea. I think I spotted Africa a
few days after that; we were far south enough. When we
get to Canada, I'll be able to say I've seen three conti-
nents. Whereas Melly will always be locked in one.

SEPTEMBER 24TH, 1870. TUTELO HEIGHTS

MOTHER AND CARRIE don't know, but in the stillness of night, I hold séances half hoping, half fearing I will hear Melly's voice again. What is it like to be dead, no longer thinking thoughts? They say hair continues growing after a person's death. Does someone measure these things? I try my best, I honestly try my best for Melly, without success. No response. Not a tipped glass or banged window or creaking furniture. No dream visitations.

How is it possible that his voice has just stopped? We agreed that whoever died first would find a way to speak that silence.

Melly, I can't hear you.

Oh god, what if it's me? Maybe he *is* talking. Maybe he's singing the Scottish National Anthem or Skinamarink or Homeward Bound, and I just can't hear.

OCTOBER 16TH, 1870. TUTELO HEIGHTS

MELLY HAS BEEN dead half a year. The silence is deafening.

OCTOBER 17TH, 1870. TUTELO HEIGHTS

I LIE in my bed or I lie on the edge of the bluff overlooking Brantford's river, and I wrap myself with rugs
and buffalo skins and pillows. Why does Mother give me
so many pillows? Father teaches his Visible Speech system at McGill University, at Harvard, at Washington
Square. Sundays I go with Mother to Service and press
my lips against her forehead and repeat the preacher's
words into her skin. But I tire of these soothsayers per-
petuating the world rather than letting it evolve. At least
Mother will never hear this preacher's voice, nasal and
lackluster. Tomorrow I plan to make an excursion to the
Six Nations Reserve. Reverend Henderson says that
although the Indians have been living side by side with
the Europeans for centuries, there is still no written version of their language. How exciting!

FEBRUARY 27TH, 1871. TUTELO HEIGHTS

MELLY HAS DESERTED me, here in this untamed land. The voice I hear inside my head is mine. Where are you Melly? has become an ironic comment on my own hearing powers, not a question at all.

The only book I brought with me from England, *On the Sensations of Tone*, I have yet to open. I've turned lazy and ineffectual. I wait every day for a letter from Father. He has promised me a teaching job in Boston. But that was months ago, and I've heard nothing. Typical! So wrapped up in his own forays he forgets me dying in this wasteland I am forced to call home.

And the company! Mother and Carrie have lost any semblance of conversation. Mother expects me to practice piano, which I can no longer stomach. She sits down herself but cannot discern a single note. Why bother? I wonder. Carrie is worse. She sits by the front window and counts carts, schoolchildren, delivery boys who pass. Every evening, she remarks on the number as if a sane person would be interested.

I must get some mathematical books—something scientific—or I will go mad from boredom.

FEBRUARY 28TH, 1871. TUTELO HEIGHTS

CARRIE ANNOUNCED today she is getting married. How is that possible? I go about town, do the shopping, greet the townspeople on my way to the Six Nations Reserve, stop for a short beer at the tavern. All Carrie does is count horses, yet she has managed to get herself engaged! Perhaps this is some Canadian courting ritual I don't yet understand?

Her fiancé insists on an April wedding. I swear that by the date of the nuptials I will be gone.

MARCH 3RD, 1871. TUTELO HEIGHTS

TODAY I VISITED Isabella Ellis at Dominion Telegraph. She ignored me while she copied out telegraphs received that morning. To gain her attention, I used Melly's trick of pulling a penny out of her ear. She looked up, then, at the stroke of my finger across her lobe. Your ear is wealthy today, I told her, pulling out another penny and another.

My sleight of hand convinced her I was worth talking to. Why must I always *prove* myself when I enter into conversation? No matter. Tomorrow we will perform an experiment, Isabella and I, and then I begin the slow process toward an invention. Mine, unlike the others, will run by electricity and the power of human utterance.

The telephone, tho' a singular idea, presupposes the existence of another.

Once I have set it firmly into this world, its spoken word will alter how we hear another's voice, will insist on the listener's reply. Will change, even, how we understand the written word.

7

Who Invented the Telephone

IN 1673, ATHANIUS KIRCHER CONSTRUCTS A MODEL of Alexander the Great's speaking trumpet. He succeeds in throwing his voice up to four miles. He builds the loudspeaker out of hammered metal and bits of willow. The two components work together to bend and amplify sound.

Robert Hooke, reporting on Boyle's famous speech transmission experiments, writes: It is possible to hear a whisper at a furlong's distance . . . and this not only in a straight line but in one bent at many angles.

Mr. Millar of Glasgow is the first to use wire to conduct sound from one locality to another. Later inventors insulate strips of these wires inside glass and support them with a thin iron diaphragm.

Sir Charles Wheatstone transmits music through wooden rods and solid wires and believes his contraptions able to project sound to distant places.

In 1837, W.B. Page replicates musical tones using galvanic currents.

Charles Bourseul announces to the French world in 1854 his intention to produce a speaking telephone. I don't see why what is spoken in Vienna might not be heard in Paris, he speculates. The thing is practical in this way . . .

By 1855, the two essential organs of the telephone have been engineered by independent inventors: the vibrating plate, which acts as transmitter, and the vibrating rod, which acts as receiver.

The missing ingredient—electricity—is soon added. Electromagnetism, M. du Moncel declares, will aid certain instruments, such as pianos. Will render them capable of being played at a distance. In order to telegraph speech, we must have the electrical ear. The power it possesses to set metallic plates into motion and cause their vibration can produce distinct sounds, which may be combined, which may be harmonized.

One inventor of the telephone, from Italy, has a monument established by the city of Aosta in his honor. The inscription reads: Innocenzo Manzetti, inventor and maker, in the year 1864, of the first telephonic apparatus.

There have been many versions of machines that reproduce irregular vibrations, especially those inventions requiring bits of wood, knitting needles or skin. By 1876, this has become a dead art.

EDWARD FARRAR, in 1851, erects two thin boards, one carrying a horseshoe magnet and the other a soft iron disk. This simple receiver is superior to Bell's first patented submission. Discouraged by a professor at Yale College, Farrar declines a test to vary the resistance of his transmitter's circuit in order that it might produce voice-wave currents. He will not be sued by the United States Bell Company.

Antonio Meucci begins experiments with the telephone in 1849 in Havana. He's too poor to take out a full patent, borrows twenty dollars to file a U.S. caveat. He submits drawings and a model to the New York District Telegraph Company president, who never tries the apparatus and loses the drawings. Meucci uses his telephone to converse from his basement study with his invalid wife on the third floor. In 1885, Meucci is successfully sued by the United States Bell Company.

M. Petrina, of Prague, builds a telephone with various keys. Currents of sound move from one instrument to another across a room. Music plays from one telephone to another through the keys. Petrina never patents the invention. He will not be sued by the United States Bell Company.

While working on lightning arrestors for a telegraph line, S.D. Cushman begins experimenting on electrical methods for transmitting sound deliberately. From 1851 to 1854, his telephones are in constant use in public areas while he attempts ways of magnifying the sound transmission so conversation can be carried on in noisy places. Cushman's transmission is faint. But Bell's telephone, at the time of its patent, has not talked at all. In 1888, Cushman is successfully sued by the United States Bell Company.

THE INVENTOR SITS alone in his study, surrounded by wires and mechanical hookups and a microphone placed in front of his lips. In another room, out of hearing range, sits the assistant. The assistant is waiting to hear whatever issues from his inventor's lips.

The inventor, anticipating failure, delays the moment of speech, fiddles with his materials, his apparatus. He touches his tongue to a thin strip of metal. It tastes bitter. The assistant sits patient. His role is that of helper, recorder. His lips will form no shapes, do not press against wire, against contraptions.

The assistant waits for the inventor to gather courage to attempt the impossible: to pass words through walls and doors and several flights of stairs. The assistant believes that he will soon hear the voice of the inventor in his ear. The assistant does not know how this will happen, though the inventor has explained the process several times. All the assistant needs to know is that he will soon hear what he cannot possibly predict.

The inventor clears the area around the microphone, leans down to speak. Earlier, he spilled some acid on his arm and cried out, but that moment was fleeting and unimportant and the assistant, set up so far away, heard nothing. The inventor feels only the dull ache at his elbow. He measures his mouth exactly two centimeters from the thin and vibrating metal, and opens his lips:

"*Pferde fressen gern Gurken Salat,*" a sentence so absurd it must be recorded accurately. Help, I need you, is what the inventor cried when he spilled the acid, which the assistant ignored because the cry did not reach his ears through the wire receiver. "*Horses prefer cucumber salad.*" This combination of nonsensical words brings the two men into the same room. Their voices convince them they are together. One speaks and the other hears. One listens while the other fabricates an entire sentence. The two men separate their physical bodies, and their words find them again.

These words travel in only one direction. The two men are not having a conversation; they do not exchange pleasantries. Philipp Reis speaks and Albert, his assistant, writes down what he hears. The assistant, the listener, walks up the three flights of stairs to Philipp Reis's laboratory and hands him a slip of paper: "*Pferde fressen gern Gurken Salat.*" An exact replica, a written account, a translation of what reached the destination of his ear.

Decades later, the Emperor of Brazil, Dom Pedro II, repeats excitedly the words, "To be or not to be," transmitted from a hundred yards away. Bell had learned well, from teaching deaf students, to choose as examples sentences or phrases with which his listeners were already acquainted.

The United States Patent Office has no physical evidence that the Reis telephone ever transmitted speech. It also has no physical evidence that the telephone Bell patented ever transmitted speech.

Philipp Reis publishes several papers on *telephony*, and his telephones spread across Europe.

Philipp Reis dies in 1874, exactly forty years after being born and almost three years before Bell submits his patent for approval. No less than four distinct varieties of the telephone are attributed to Reis.

Both the inventor and his assistant understand that they are at the mercy of the ear. The ear and the mouth. Philipp Reis, who gives the contraption its name, looks forward to the day when such a transmitter will also involve the eye.

Philipp Reis is a school teacher. He desires to expand his students' world by offering them the spoken word. He absents himself from the classroom and iterates into his machine one sentence of the day's lecture. His students look up into the air, trying to locate sound.

Now, he says to the heads swiveling to catch his voice, do you *see?*

THE NARRATOR RECALLS PROFESSOR REIS:

When I turn twelve, my mother takes me to her—and Philipp Reis's—home town. I meet my *Oma* and *Opa*, with whom I have only talked long distance. Although born in northern Germany, *Mutti* grew up in Friedrichs-dorf where Reis lived and taught. I go to the Philipp Reis high school and visit his house, now a museum. I still have the black-and-white photos showing each stage of Reis's invention.

The townspeople here do not connect the name Bell with the modern telephone.

8

Naked in Your Body

Don't think Bell wasn't a hero. He was a hero, all right, just not in his own country.

After the family settles in Tutelo Heights, Aleck goes out to the Six Nations Reserve to extract new sounds for his father's system of recording Visible Speech. He is intrigued by the vision of himself inventing writing. He wants to be seduced by a virgin language.

The first man Aleck meets reaches a hand up, not out, for a handshake. Aleck misunderstands meaning, doesn't read the gesture as greeting. The man takes a step closer to Aleck, offers him a name and tells him this smoky day is swollen with appetite. Aleck misunderstands meaning. When this man speaks, he sings, and Aleck registers only lilts and rhythms.

Aleck explains his project. I want to transcribe your words, he says. He shows his notebook and the strange squiggles there that mean sound. The singer doesn't glance at Aleck's notebook but points him in the direction of other voices. Aleck joins a circle of cross-legged men and waits for them to speak. The men in this group greet each other with the stroke of thumb against moccasin. The singer joins the circle and passes both his palms underneath the chins of his neighbors. Aleck waits patiently. He witnesses layers of unspoken ritual. He writes nothing down in his book. He waits. A pipe passes his chest, but he is not offered a puff.

Years later Aleck will remember a wrinkled set of fingers stroking the long tube of this pipe or young fingers braiding hair. But he will have no written words preserving these pictures. Years later, isolated details will leap at him unexpectedly. Disembodied images. The tight swirl of smoke released from lips. The braided thongs of a leather shirt. An elbowed jawline.

At this moment, Aleck only notices the expectant blankness of the pages in his Thought Book. "Visible Speech. Iroquois," he writes down at the top left-hand corner. And the date.

Aleck the boy taught his dog to growl a sentence in English. He witnessed automatons who could cheat at chess. Aleck the adult wants to make something of himself. How would it be, he thinks while waiting for this circle of people to form their tongues around trapped breath, how would it be to invent talking?

The singer rests the tip of the pipe against an indent in his chin and closes his eyes. Aleck holds his pencil at the ready. The singer refuses to exhale the smoke contained in his lungs. All the other people stop breathing. Aleck's own lungs constrict in sympathetic vibration. Like Melly's piano when I sing to it, Aleck thinks. He still can't convince his body to relax into release rhythm. He's forgotten the melody of breathing, can only pitch himself to the exact note of the controlled and unyielding example of this man.

The singer, still refusing to exchange smoke for air,

raises his body from a squat to a full standing position, legs still crossed at the knees, as if holding a secret. Aleck feels prickles in his own legs and bum. The singer pivots on his heels, his legs uncross themselves and he removes himself from the circle. In one simultaneous rush of breath, the seated people relax their diaphragms, the noise of this so close to the sound of laughter that Aleck scribbles for several seconds before his lungs contract and his body remembers to inhale.

He writes the laughter, a page of belly rumbles. But he wants more. He wants to follow the singer, but Aleck isn't confident his knees can perform that trick. The men in the circle have begun passing the pipe again, reaching past Aleck. The thing is, Aleck isn't an adult. He's mostly child, pretending adult games. So it isn't entirely his fault that he misunderstands what comes next. Misunderstands what he later names his victory dance.

The only gesture Aleck can bring himself to substitute for the spoken word is to point with one index finger to his ear and to point with the other index finger to another speaker's mouth. These Mohawks, too, misinterpret Aleck. Although rudimentary, the men still observing the circle think they perceive signs imbedded in Aleck's crude beckonings. They believe his fingers invite them to dance the dance of arms and mouths, and of seeing what another person sees with closed eyes. They understand Aleck's fingers to point in the direction of desire and that he wants, with them, to become telephones.

One by one, people pair off. With others who have come to join in but don't sit in the circle, with some of the children, younger than Aleck himself. Aleck stands in front of a much older woman, already hunched and squatted into position. The couples around him begin inserting their index fingers into each other's ears. One finger. Then another. They squat or kneel, stare penetratingly into another pair of eyes. Aleck misunderstands. He believes he is witnessing another layer of ritual, but really these people are dancing. Dancing news. Dancing stories. Aleck tries to ignore his partner. Right in front of him, the old woman sways. One shoulder higher than the other, but her swaying still balanced, even. She doesn't hum. No, her body transforms into an instrument to convey sound. Or music. She is waiting for Aleck to tune in to the flow of her blood, for him to want to listen to what her skin has to say. Aleck, brushing her fingers out of his ears, refuses this game. Refuses this old woman penetrating the inside of how his body sounds. She doesn't try to insert her fingers into his ear holes again. She is not persistent, only hopeful. Why would a young man refuse the advances of experience? Of delicate manual intercourse? Aleck, not looking down, not looking ahead, walks the road home to Tutelo Heights. The very last person he sees on the reserve is the first man he met.

I've written a breath song about this, the man says to Aleck, but you wouldn't understand a word of it, not one word.

9

Speak Loudly to the Deaf

A DEBATE ARISES IN THE MASSACHUSETTS LEGISLATURE.

For her fifth birthday, Mabel Hubbard's mother takes her on a train to New York, a city that should be a song because its name rhymes with itself. May's mother's mother lives in New York, New York. A twin city of mirrored doubles. May likes twins that don't look alike at all but really are. May has another name and lives in Cambridge, which is in Boston. Inside Cambridge lives a bridge, which goes over water or other bridges, depending where you put it. Once they reach New York, she turns into a girl from Boston: a city inside a city inside something else altogether.

The backers of this debate, the rigorous supporters of teaching speech to Mutes, include Samuel Gridley Howe—a politician addicted to the struggle of reform, and Gardiner Greene Hubbard—a rich Bostonian businessman who had managed, in spite of his prominent social status, to beget a deaf child.

In New York, May suffers scarlet fever. Her forehead fluctuates from hot to hot to hot. Not just her eardrums, but her eyes and nostrils burst from energy disturbing the openings. May screams and screams until her throat clogs together, refusing to be passageway, until her ears no longer process her scream as voice. Her mother sits by the bed, strokes ice chips over skin that devours solid water.

Howe walks into the Legislature with Hubbard on his shoulder. The two men beg for deaf students to be given the opportunity to become like every other person. How can we deny Mutes the right to appear normal, Howe pleads. If we do not teach Mutes to read English on the lips of Americans, how can they fit into our world? The two men flood the House, drowning the rows of seated men with examples of deaf adults who can speak. They don't bother to explain that these deaf adults have only relatively recently lost the ability to hear. Not one of their shining examples was born deaf. Howe doesn't mention this. Slips his tongue.

Mabel Hubbard is totally deaf. May-the-deaf-girl. Until age seven May sings songs to herself: Peter Pumpkin, Ring Around the Rosy, Away in a Manger. May plays toy soldier and tea party and school-in-a-real-classroom. She recites her sisters' names: Sister-the-oldest, Berta, Grace, Marian-the-baby, and Carrie-Dwyer-who-lives-next-door. May is the second-oldest daughter. She holds and coddles the sisters until they squirm away from her arms, until she loses the knack of words.

BUT, stands up one dissenter from the rear of the Legislature seats, BUT, he speaks out from far away, his seat at the back too far for any eye to catch the lipswirl of protest, BUT, everyone hears his voice travel far and above the other deciding heads, BUT, an interruption of the Howe/Hubbard presentation on how well deaf children will soon speak as if they're not deaf at all. BUT.

What about math-science-history-literature-geography-classics-music? BUT. Shouldn't articulation skills be an adornment, rather than the basis of instruction? BUT. Funny how the spoken voice can be ignored even when the ears function. Funny how the Hearing will sometimes turn a deaf ear.

May's tongue already knows how to twist itself around *th*s and *ch*s. There is no biological reason not to continue speaking. But her lips form themselves less and less confidently around vowels, and her consonants slur and distort. May's vocabulary stubbornly refuses to expand. To hear her speak, one might guess she'd been born deaf. Gardiner Greene Hubbard rejects this handicap.

BEFORE TAKING on the cause of Oralism, Samuel Gridley Howe:

- argues in favor of state reform schools
- argues for prison reform
- fights *against* the immediate abolishment of slavery
- fights *for* the abolishment of slavery
- supports the Cretin revolt in Greece against the Turks
- carries funds for Polish revolutionaries in Prussia
- returns to Boston, exiled from Prussia, to direct the newly opened Perkins Institute for the Blind

IF YOU WANT your daughter to be normal, Howe tells Hubbard, you must speak to her and she must speak to you.

But May's speech continues to deteriorate. Her parents only allow her to play with her sisters. Her parents only allow her to meet other hearing children. Her parents hire a governess. Her parents slap May's hands when she signs or attempts hand gestures of any kind. May lives in a world she creates out of her childhood.

May's father needs to hear his daughter perform the spoken. Needs, even more, for others to hear this ordinary miracle. A young lady who doesn't speak might be deemed mysterious, desirable, clever even. But a young lady who can't talk might be thought Dumb.

By the time the Perkins Institute is financially established, Howe has already stumbled on to his latest cause: Deaf people are sorely left out of society, he reasons, having never talked to a deaf person. Having never met a deaf person. And children who sign invite the danger of neglecting precious oral skills because of their unnatural dependency on pantomime. Howe, with financial and moral backing from Hubbard, approaches the Legislature with an appeal to bring all deaf children to his school for the blind. The school, he promises the House, will establish classes in speech and lipreading only.

Miss-True-the-governess practices lipreading with May all day. In the morning, May writes down what Miss True's lips tell her, and in the afternoon, May forces her own lips to pulse out sound. Any sound. All the sound she can remember. May even likes this game, although she doesn't understand it. She remembers that lip-flapping has something to do with the way you can point to a speckled stone in the river or see your sister's face when she's not in the same room. But May no longer makes any connection between that time of hearing and her governess pressing her face so closely into May's own.

The Perkins Institute for the Blind begins advertising for deaf students. But they need to prove this will not be an added expense for the Massachusetts Legislature. Howe sets up a policy to employ Untrained Females to teach articulation. They teach out of love, he tells his board, not because of the salary. Deaf children, he tells his Board, only require enough mouths to stare at. One-on-one, every day, every day. One teacher, one student, cheap at the price, he tells his Board, cheap at the price.

Although May manages to read certain words, she cannot decipher their meaning. Miss-True-the-governess was a missionary's daughter before the Hubbards hire her to instruct May full-time. She taught Bible studies and religious worship to the children of the wealthy. Over and over, Miss True points to a word in the Bible so May will mouth each letter. May can say the alphabet every time because it's also a song. Miss True ignores how to explain silent letters. She lets the child pronounce them anyway, correcting only when May forgets that the gap between words indicates closure and swallows her endings.

The point of learning, for May, has become making the correct mouth shapes in order to please Miss True to please her father. But these tongue exercises have no meaning for her. May's sisters read the same words. Nobody stares at their lips; nobody grabs their chins, tilts their heads up at a grown-up set of flapping lips. Her sisters open their mouths and run at the same time out of the playroom. Her sisters hide from each other, yet always know when to come out, come out wherever they are. May plays Miss True's lip game very seriously. Somehow through this lip-flapping she will be able to meet her sisters' friends and play games that have more than one verse in them. Somehow, May understands, she should be learning how to hear.

TWO DEAF PUPILS FACE each other in a classroom in the Perkins Institute for the Blind. They rehearse lipreading. A girl describes the landscape outside, and her fingers stretch toward the window. A teacher raps her knuckles, and the wounded hand slides back into her lap. For who has control of a classroom if the students all speak in a language of which their teachers are ignorant?

The second pupil, a boy two years older, avoids looking where her finger points. If he lets his eyes slip from her lips he will never catch up, never manage to repeat this description back to the teacher.

Tree, the girl says at him. Tease? Deal? Tea? Rocks? Her lips aim for perfection. Walk? Rude? The boy cannot unearth the world inside her mouth. He longs to reach out, grab her words and stuff them into his eyes.

The boy has the sick feeling that he will begin to cry. And if he cries, the tears will drown his vision.

The girl promises to her smarting fingers that she will not gesture again. The sign for sun as obvious as releasing the fist in her lap. But she knows the boy will not lower his eyes. Not for even an instant of borrowed sunshine.

The girl watches the boy's lips flap a reply. She smiles. She caught one word. Play. She says it back at him, and he repeats it again to her. They go on like this, passing solitary words back and forth until the other has caught it squarely between the lips. One by one, word by word. The teacher can't lip-read, so she doesn't follow this fractured discourse. Not many of the teachers understand the gnarled sounds that pass as speech. When the teacher quizzes this girl, this boy, after their exercise, both will speak the same words.

MAY'S FATHER BELIEVES that association makes the deaf deafer, the dumb dumber. May has never met another deaf child. She doesn't know that adults can be deaf, too. Her father tries so hard, and she still hasn't learned how to hear. Sometimes her sisters run off together without warning, and then May is alone. She wanders the huge garden and talks to the daisies. The daisies bow their heads in greeting. May has long, involved conversations about how much they've grown today, how much of their skin the bees have stolen, if he loves her. The daisies don't expect May to read their lips. She stares down at them and hears their petals caress air. The pinks so much louder than the yellows. Or purples. May remembers how a certain color can sing a note or vibrate the scales of a piano. She remembers the sound a bird's wing makes when it hugs sky. Her eyes remind her that a snail can make noise losing its shell. A scream that tears her insides in two.

GROOMING FOR A YOUNG LADY in Boston: the basis for education. May's father hires another governess, this time to teach his daughter how to walk up steps or carry an umbrella in sunshine or laugh with her mouth closed. May has never had a dainty laugh. She is forced, these days, to spend every afternoon indoors rehearsing strategies of poise. Her steady companion is a matron whose seven daughters have all married prominent businessmen. But all seven daughters have mastered speech and hearing, and May is beginning to understand that she never will. Marriage, according to her father, is the only destination possible. And for her, the only goal impossible. For months and months she is trapped in the parlor folding handkerchiefs and removing her gloves one finger at a time, her eyes gray with boredom. For the first time in her life, May considers mutiny. There was a time, after her illness, when she could still hear the dependable and deadly sound of her father's voice. But that reverberation is now only memory.

Sixteen, and May stops believing in voice. Hers. Ugly and unpleasant. I'm not going to talk anymore, she announces to her father. Gardiner Hubbard takes out his pipe and makes her repeat the sentence. Say it clearly, May, he says. Inflection, that's the key. If I need to, May persists, I will use a pencil and paper. Impress young men with my exquisite handwriting. The word exquisite pleases her father. Say it again, May, put more muscle into the X. My voice, Father, will only reduce the likelihood of marriage.

Getting married—now that she has figured out she will never hear again, now that she listens to the story of her voice as fiction—is the only gift May has to offer her father.

When Hubbard suggests a new speech therapist, an articulation specialist willing to take on private pupils, May refuses. No. I'm done with this talking business, she writes. I want the world back. She hands him the paper, keeps her lips firmly together. No more tiny rooms and staring at bad teeth and lip sores. No more hours spent on the letter *Q*. Her father hands back the paper and pencil. I can hear perfectly well without sound, May writes. Mr. Hubbard refuses to read the sentence.

May, unable to bear her father's silence, her father's refusal to accept her refusal, agrees to this teacher, agrees to Alexander Graham Bell. He's the last one, she says. For the last time, for this last man, I'll mimic speech.

10

Because Wood, so too Metal

MUSICIANS RELY ON AN INSTRUMENT'S MEMORY.

A cello played only by one master, so well and for so long, will bend into a groove of expectation. The wood itself molded by the perfect concerto. Again and again, the same notes, the same lyrical pattern, so that even an amateur will discover sweet half notes inside such impressionable instruments. The wood remembers, inspires perfection.

Aleck has listened to piano wires that hum sympathetic accompaniment to a perfectly pitched voice. For months he has pursued the prospect of the multiple telegraph. He has set up contradicting experiments a hundred times and inside each failure has discovered easily one hundred more to follow. The path to the telegraph, though it forks away from the idea of the straight line, is clearly there. Aleck needs to discover the method of discovery.

But the telegraph no longer interests him. The telegraph is a mechanical proposition that excludes the human voice. Gardiner Greene Hubbard, who sponsors Aleck, invested in this likely invention. He believes in the multiple telegraph because Aleck has insisted it will work. Hubbard is unaware that Aleck has been seduced by voice, by the possibility that these wires might remember what has been spoken into them.

Metal may be pliable as wood. A mechanical instrument is still an instrument.

Aleck leans down over his dismantled telegraph contraption, sings into its wires. He will perform this miracle every day, coating the instrument with the rhythm of his song. Aleck hopes the wires will listen to his voice. Will become haunted by the imperceptible echo he has managed to imprint on this copper alloy. Even a fly can distort the straight line that is a metal rod. Aleck wants these utensils to memorize sound.

ALECK BREAKS away from his singing when he can no longer hear the exact pitch of his voice, when the sound that issues from his mouth is so distorted to his ears that he fears he may warp the wires. He thrusts his hat on his head and grabs his walking stick. The walking stick is to improve upon the shabby appearance of his clothes. On his way down the stairs, he bumps into Watson, a man deaf to the intricacies of musical notes and timbres, a man who has arrived because he desires to work in the vision-ary field of electronics. Aleck brushes by this stranger, a watcher whose weekly pay packet should guarantee an interest in multiple taps and clicks across a telegraph wire. The stranger's path could only be a direct line toward the apartment Aleck just quit. But Aleck needs air against his ears and the regular sounds of horses clopping through the streets. The odd banging, the swish of clothing against the boardwalk. He needs to remember what the world sounds like before he traps it inside a piece of machinery.

Watson, though, recognizes this young man. After being ignored, Watson proceeds to the top step to await Aleck's return. Hubbard instructed Watson that Aleck specifically requested services. Watson doesn't yet under-stand the layers of betrayal these two will ask him to per-form. The multiple versions of truth he will learn to speak at the same time.

By the time Aleck returns to his apartment, Watson will have picked the lock. Watson's hands can persuade any machine to do what he tells it. He picks the lock and swings the door wide open. Inside its frame, Aleck dis-covers a man asleep. Watson wants Aleck to recognize him as the perfect assistant: capable of the mechanical skill to further his own entrance into the inventor's world.

Aleck stands there. Weary from his experiments, vocal chords aching, he does not know what to do with this new person insinuated into his life. There is his mother, and there is Mabel. Outside that circle there is his father, and there is Gardiner Greene Hubbard. This stranger, who trusts himself to fall asleep inside another man's home, doesn't fit Aleck's concentric pattern.

At least he's silent, Aleck thinks.

Watson is up and dusting the sleep out of his eyes, and Aleck sits silently in the kitchen waiting for water to boil so he can make tea. He has closed the door to his work room. There is no need for him to hold back words, but he hasn't yet decided what to say to Watson, whether to accept Hubbard's deviation from their signed agreement. He cannot afford to become more grateful to the man. But he cannot afford to turn away eager assistants either.

Watson leans against the doorframe. He prefers to position himself between rooms rather than inside them, a form of spatial fence-sitting. He abstains from talking. He has offered himself to this young inventor once, now has the patience to swallow extra words. Aleck needs him. Watson assumed this from the first moment he opened his eyes to witness a man who didn't know whether to step over or on him. A man caught in his own hesitant desire.

What Aleck wants or how he expects to achieve this want is beyond Watson. Still, Watson believes he can help. He suspends himself in the doorway, wordless and solemn, until Aleck begins to believe, too.

ALECK DOESN'T TRUST Watson. They work separately, Watson in one room with the now defunct telegraph apparatus and Aleck enclosed in his bedroom serenading his metal strips. Every day, Watson materializes whenever Aleck chooses to open the door. He never knocks. Aleck cannot catch him in the act of arrival. Watson is either there or not-there.

Aleck grabs the door, hurtles it open. Nobody. Or else: his new assistant, propped there against the door frame in a pose of quiet resignation. Even if Aleck props the door open to trap Watson's footsteps, he is defeated in capturing even an echo. His ears strain against his own breathing, and then there will be Watson, looming above Aleck's worktable, waiting for the gesture that will invite him inside.

Aleck doesn't yet know Watson's first name.

The two begin to schedule their work. Watson appears later in the afternoon, sets up equipment while Aleck completes his last day's speech lesson. Watson unrolls hand diagrams to the tune of *ah, ah, ah* or checks his module frequency to the *ph, ph, ph* of expired air. When the last deaf student is gone, the two attack the workbench in a synchronized progress of chaos. They understand the principal of multiple clicks on the telegraph wire. They believe the system can be collapsed into one continuous strand of pitch. But their methods divorce each other.

In the Williams' machine shop where he still works, Watson is now assigned exclusively to inventors. Only he, of all the assistants, can take the poetry of beam pulleys or brass sheets and make a practice out of them. The customers trust him to tell them how an idea in their heads might be turned into a contraption they can operate. But Aleck doesn't want explanations on how a thing can work. He just wants it to happen.

Me, I'd use liquid on the thing, Watson suggests.

Don't begin a sentence with a predicate pronoun, is Aleck's only reply.

Metal and water and electricity, says Watson. Could be an explosion.

Aleck stares down the metal, clicking his tongue in disapproval at every mathematical deviation. Watson wanders the room. His feet cover the wooden cracks and knots Aleck's rug is too poor to conceal. He clamps his lips together, and his eyes blink when he stares at the pictures Aleck has saved from Scotland. His eyes trace the route of the telegraph wires along the cracks in the wall.

Vision, Watson says to Aleck who ignores his chatter, can also reproduce sound.

ALECK'S ROOMS are decorated sparsely. Watson gradually introduces bits of himself to the apartment. Aleck cannot say when the first hint of green intrudes into the dusty attic. Watson must have washed the windows; Aleck never saw the spiderwebs before. Bits of colored ribbons hang from the windowsills.

The attic's corners are littered with what Aleck assumes is rubble, but Watson explains that the rocks are specimens he has collected: Malachite. Jasper. Cat's eye. Dull earth tones that litter the floors. Iceland spar. Willemite calcite from Quebec. Tinstone. Aleck swears he will break his neck stepping over these overgrown pebbles.

Watson's planted herbs and spices sprout wherever the sun can reach. Each has a tiny white stick inserted into the earth with a name printed up one side. Basil and cloves and mace and caraway. Each still a minuscule growth on Aleck's window ledge. One ginger stalk, red and bewitching. The gathering foreign scents, carried inside on the Boston air, assault Aleck's logic. He tastes dried peppermint leaf crumpled on his tongue.

THE THREE OF THEM in the same room: Aleck, Watson, Mabel. Today Watson appears before Aleck's last session with his newest student had concluded. Or Mabel arrives early for a lesson while Aleck and Watson still bend over the latest gadget. Aleck has taken to changing his work hours because his regular teaching lectures and the idiosyncrasies of his various students and their wealthy parents do not invite a healthy workday. Aleck expects this to entangle or annoy Watson. He expects Watson to lobby for more respectable hours. Instead of this constant wild rotation: 7:00 A.M. 11:30 P.M. 2:00 P.M. 3:30 A.M. But Watson fits into Aleck's time slots the way he fits herbs and spices onto the attic's crowded floors. Now: Watson and Mabel, two unknown integers.

There. Watson has made Mabel laugh. Her laugh shrill, she loses a lot of air. Aleck hears that her nasal passages are too open, that she must learn to breathe less when she finds some prank funny. Watson points to his thumb and pinkie finger, then to his nose. Mabel laughs again, and Aleck hears her vocal cords straining to close. Next lesson they will work only on her laugh. He will draw a diagram in Visible Speech for her of what that sound looks like, help her remember how to imitate her own laughter. Imitation. Adaptation. Protective coloring.

Learn to hear what you sound like, he tells his pupils. Then learn to change that sound. He teaches them the Hearing World's camouflage.

MABEL BENDS over Watson's shoulders and traces his lips. Her finger travels across his cheek, his neck, down his shoulder and arm. He has rolled his shirt-sleeves past his elbows. Mabel stops where shirt meets skin. His arm remains perfectly still, expressing an invitation. She stares down at his forearms, reaches to stroke the hairs, finds a thick vein, follows it. Then traces another back to his elbow again. She looks up at his face, expecting to see lips flapping at her, instruction she will not be able to follow. But Watson has closed his eyes, and his lips signal nothing. She stares at his closed lids a long time before she removes her hand from his. Then she steps away from the workbench and goes to sit beside her teacher.

What would you like me to say? she asks Aleck, and her lips ache each vowel. But Aleck is too aware of Watson's arm on the table, Watson's eyes closed against this scene. Aleck senses Watson not looking. He offers the crook of his arm and leads Mabel Hubbard to a chair directly opposite his own. Mabel has permitted Aleck this interruption of the conversation.

WATSON IS NOT around the next time Mabel shows up for her lesson.

Aleck runs through the drills of Visible Speech, teaches her three new variables and draws small ticks beside each letter to indicate the exceptions. Mabel doesn't understand the exceptions. They squirm out from underneath her tongue. She can't sense the word anymore. She has no patience for the ridiculous. And the precision of these exercises displays no beauty. But she has promised her father, and so she works diligently, making words out of air and the shape of her jaw. The other one isn't here this time. She has never been so bold as to stroke a man's skin before. To stroke anyone's skin. And now that she's touched him, he's disappeared. If she asked Professor Bell, would he tell her if the man will return? No, her new instructor will only tolerate articulation questions. What would be the point in Mabel proposing a question merely for the sake of its answer? She sighs. Aleck hears the boredom.

Aleck stashes the Visible Speech charts under his chair, invents a game for Mabel. He feels like a magician, waves a ruler over his head, and Mabel has to say whatever he points to. She is sluggish to begin with, then picks up when she realizes that he isn't stopping for mispronunciations. Aleck's interest is in the momentum Mabel achieves when she forgets that she can't hear.

la-amp, Mabel says. kRa-kR. Her words slur around his apartment, stop wherever his wooden pointer does. stul. ke-tL. pi-chur frA-Am. tI-Im.

No. Aleck says, clock. Two *kh* sounds. The second one half swallowed. Say it, Mabel. Clock.

Time.

No. Clock, he says. Again.

Time.

Thyme: beside the clock, Watson's tiny plant. Not even an inch high. But Mabel knows its name.

II

The Thought Books of A. Graham Bell

NOVEMBER 2ND, 1872. BOSTON

WATSON HAS PROVEN HIMSELF A GODSEND, yet I don't trust the man. He is a good worker but eternally tired. I have caught him napping several times this past week, asleep with his arms wrapped around his ears. Oblivious. There's work to be done, I say loudly enough, but sometimes even that won't rouse him. He sleeps in his chair and on my work table, and once he fell asleep in the middle of fixing a leaky pipe. I strode into the kitchen in search of black tea and discovered his legs sticking out of my cupboard. He could have been a dead body. He has yet to offer me an explanation or apology.

Watson loves the deafness of sleep too much.

NOVEMBER 13TH, 1872. BOSTON

RATHER THAN TAKING the train back to Salem every night, Watson has been sleeping on my floors. Watson is handy and young. His head brims with ideas that help my own, my mechanical man-Friday, tho' his yearning for magic leads him away from the path of science. Watson believes electricity to be an occult force and listens, fascinated, to what he calls the music of static.

But I cannot bear living with a man so mannerless. He shovels food down his throat without stopping his conversation. He rolls his sleeves up and turns chairs wrong side around in order to dine. He holds his knife in a fist, stabs at his food, then pokes the whole thing into his mouth. He eats as if he has never been introduced to a fork. I am disgusted every meal. What can I do?

Yesterday I burst out: Were you born in a barn? and without pause or hesitation, he replied: Yes, my father ran the stables.

What can I make of that? Watson slips food inside his mouth with a dexterity that comes from necessity. Too busy swallowing, he lacks conversation skills at the table. I, too, increase the speed of my food intake and soon enough we are back in the attic speaking to each other through metal and wires.

NOVEMBER 28TH, 1872. BOSTON

I CAN'T fathom Hubbard's motives. He sponsors my scientific endeavors financially, sends his daughter to me, assuming I can perform a miracle of speech with her, yet directs and manipulates my experiments, understanding nothing. Money, of course, but there is more money to be had in creating a machine that can talk than in merely encouraging simultaneous telegraphs. Hubbard pushes so hard for the telegraph invention, and it is, after all, his funding that pays for the equipment and for the attic suite and for Watson, but I cannot bear to be the first person to develop a contraption only to watch it turn obsolete in days.

Invention is about voice and where I can send it. Hubbard, a businessman, doesn't understand this seduction's about changing the future. Being original doesn't count for much; Hubbard should know that. What counts is the forward leap. The hesitation between connections.

The multiple telegraph is obsolete already, yet Hubbard insists I spend hours a day searching for ways to invent the thing. Fool.

I want to trap the human throat inside a box. I want to speak to Watson without tolerating his body in the same room. I want Mabel Hubbard to implant my device inside her ear.

The future, I have discovered, is no longer what it used to be.

DECEMBER 23RD, 1872. BOSTON

THE BEST KISS I ever had I can't remember.

Marie and I walking—no hiking—I felt so sorry for her limp, for her inability to climb rocks or scale mountains.

Marie always endeavored to scale mountains.

I followed her footsteps on the steep path then increased my gait so I could accompany her bad leg. An injury or birth defect, she never said. And I wanted so wickedly to help, to offer a bent elbow, to wrap an arm around her waist. To lift.

Really, I wanted to touch her, her lameness the excuse I invented. But Marie refused to understand her lameness. She hobbled and scrambled over that difficult path more eager than I. She turned, and I froze my arm against my chest in order not to reach for hers. I wanted to touch her. My fingers consumed with desire to stretch out against skin. My body, caught between its own longing and her resistance, unable to follow either path.

She kissed me then. While my hand hesitated solo above her unafraid arm, she kissed me open mouthed and full against my greedy surprise.

I kissed her back, of course, her tongue sensational and confident beneath my own. I pulled her inside my lips and tried to trap her breath there beneath my tongue. I can't remember, but the dynamite persuasion of her mouth gasping against mine resonates inside my body.

An explosion.

My body reminds me it was too convenient, Marie's kiss, and too much hoped for. A kiss I will try to memorize all my life. The best kiss I ever. The best I ever.

JANUARY 3RD, 1873. BOSTON

MABEL'S MOUTH smells of apples and birch trees. A
New England mouth twists around *k*s and *t*s and
breathes out even and confident. Mabel claims she can
read my lips, but I don't believe her. I mouth: I-love-
you-I-love-you-I-love—. She can't hear. She turns away
from my overzealous lips and cradles the caraway seeds
on the windowsill. Look, she says into the glass, the
shells are invisible.

I used to breathe words against my mother's forehead.
My mother couldn't decipher a single sound except by me
pressing my lips against her receptive temple. My mother, who has never heard my father speak her name, has
heard her one remaining son sing churchly hymns,
expound on the Great Beyond. Although no lover of reli-
gion, I plucked sermons and diatribes from the air above
my mother, pushed them into her head. Her skull
remembers what she can no longer hear. My mother
stares at the minister every Sunday—every Sunday for
forty-one years with only one change of country in
between—but cannot discern what his lips trace. She
misses the singing, my mother says. She misses the long
hollow words retreating into exile.

Mabel claims she has no need to hear. She turns from
the clear glass, lowers her eyes, stares at the motion of my
lips.

I lean my shoulders forward: -love-you-I-love-you-I-
love-you-I—my lips rehearse silently, so Watson in the
next room can't hear. Mabel can't hear. The final -I-
catches in my throat, and I choke on words that even I
can't hear.

Mabel concentrates on my lips and sees sound. What sort of hearing, then, can I put into her eyes? Or might Watson outline from across the room where I don't notice?

Mabel claims she can read lips, but I say differently.

JANUARY 31ST, 1875. BOSTON

I CAN'T stand this infernal heat. How is it possible to be suffering from sweat in the middle of winter? Even Ontario makes more sense than this country.

Watson and I enter the attic, strip down to our trousers and bare skin, and immediately begin to over-heat. We keep the windows closed so the air doesn't disturb the passage of sound through wires. It gets so bad, we go down to the kitchen just to breathe to the bottom of our lungs. Watson finds it impossible to stay awake for large spaces of time when working in the attic. I usually send him down to make the tea. Otherwise, when I return with a boiling pot of chamomile or Earl Grey, I'll find him slumped over the connectors, drowsing into an amplifier. It's too hot to drink the stuff, but I send Watson anyway. He slumbers against the counter until the kettle's whine wakes him, then comes back upstairs refreshed.

The logistics of this thing wind round and round my head. I can't grab hold of the angles. Hubbard wants his telegraph. Father wants me to continue with his Visible Speech system. I've yet to hear of Father using his method to teach his own wife.

Mabel claims that lipreading is possible. To Mabel, anything is possible. Why doesn't Mother think that way? Mabel stares at my lips, which frees me to stare at her. For someone so young, Mabel is tough. Her parents never let her grow up Deaf, so she isn't; she's a hearing person gone deaf. She is the shining example I show off to my other deaf pupils' parents. Look, I tell them. If this girl can learn to speak, so can your daughters, so will your sons.

And they believe me.

Those with money entrust their children to me, but I no longer make personal time for instructing such individuals. I feel like a circus entertainer whose juggling balls rest on the ground. What happened to my delicate balance?

Mabel arrives early for her lesson and flirts with Watson until I send him away. They are both children, still.

12

Husha-Husha

RECITE ONE OF YOUR OLD NURSERY RHYMES, Aleck lips at Mabel. Perhaps memory will trigger in this girl the urge to speak normally. She is his most promising and most difficult student. The years and years her parents have invested in her articulation have turned her against the beauty of sound.

Children, Aleck knows, need encouragement.

Sing to me, he says to her again and opens his own mouth wide as if in accompaniment. She believes he is singing with her. Astounded, Aleck hears Mabel repeat flawlessly the lilt and cadence of Ring Around the Rosy. Her voice, harsh and untrained and forgotten, startles him with its accuracy. She can no longer pronounce the rhymes, but the idea of the melody resides in her memory.

Mabel, had she not gone deaf with scarlet fever, would have a perfect ear. Childhood tunes beat beneath her skull. Another, he says to her when the song ends. One more, one more, each time she closes her lips.

Mabel has never met anyone who likes the noise her throat makes.

Aleck's fingers twitch against the sides of his legs as if he must restrain himself from reaching out and plucking her voice out of air. Mabel opens her lips and sings. Another. And another. She stares at Aleck's hands and makes stories out of the thick workman fingers and the chipped and gritty nails. From his hands, she knows he is more than a teacher or statesman.

Mabel's voice wavers along the walls and ceilings; her hands rest on Aleck's undulating fingers. This is their first lesson together where he hasn't worn gloves.

Mabel tells Aleck that except for her immediate family she talks to no one. She writes this down so that he will understand her exactly. Aleck wonders if she writes notes to the grocer and to delivery boys. He multiplies her opportunities for befriending.

Perhaps Mabel has met Watson before. Perhaps in hiring Watson, her father employed a family acquaintance, a man Mabel must surely have met previously? Mabel's index finger traces Watson's forearm. She removes her white gloves one finger at a time and reaches her hand to the sleeping Watson, a man consumed by the urge to close his eyes in front of strangers.

Child's play, Aleck thinks, observing the two of them. Watson and Mabel remember games and toys too well. Both are on the other side of twenty from Aleck. Watson thinks the task of invention jolly good fun; Mabel deigns to receive the benefits of speech for the sake of her father. Two children, Aleck thinks.

Mabel has invented the art of reading lips. And Watson has invented layers upon layers of improved defunct telephones.

FOR THE DURATION of the invention of the telephone, Watson must fit his life into Aleck's. Watson is his and his alone. That Watson has a full-time position as a mechanic in someone else's shop is an irritation to Aleck. Watson works in the attic before he goes to the shop, after he goes to the shop. In the middle of the night, he arrives from Salem and works until morning. Watson sleeps on the train, he sleeps on the trams to and from Aleck's home, he sleeps on the desk when a space of five minutes opens up and Aleck is late with a deaf student. His day is divided into snatches of naps, sections of dreams that never reach their end. He wakes from a twenty-minute snooze, his hands already wrapped around the base of a telegraph wire. His body, pushed and strained, prepares to steal seconds of night.

Asleep or awake, Watson is the same person.

Aleck walks into the apartment, stares at his young assistant's lanky legs, sprawled between two rooms, oblivious to the approaching day.

On his one day off a month, Watson doesn't ride home to Salem, doesn't retreat to his bunk to sleep the sleep of twenty-nine days of never enough sleep. No. On his only free day, on this one day in thirty that he can designate his own, Watson takes the train out of Boston.

When the train passes over Lynn marshes, Watson focuses his attention outside the car window. He should shut his eyes. He should lean back and rest his head against the window and invest these few moments of his free day in healing his exhausted body. But Watson is a young man, practically a boy. The risk of the day still tastes fresh in his lungs.

When they first met, Aleck told Watson his name was

Graham Bell, and that's what Watson called him for weeks. Watson now wishes he'd offered his own middle name, Augustus, as fair exchange. Watson hadn't understood Aleck's obsession with titles. Aleck has a nickname for Mabel that Watson can't bear to repeat: Adored One. Luckily, Watson thinks, Mabel can't hear the sugar tones reverberate inside the cracks of the inventor's lips. She reads Joan of Arc there, or she shuts her eyes.

The sun low on the horizon, Watson stares at the liquid shimmer of the field. The train's shadow bends and darts about the creases in the landscape, and Watson locates his own shadow inside its trace. He focuses on an elongated glow, a little brighter than the sunlight on the grass, that marks where he's seated. He changes seats, and the wavering halo follows him. He walks the length of the car until he stands at the train's end platform. The glow is there, too. Watson is astounded. Is this a flag of today's foolhardiness or some divine communication? The halo surely streams from his head! He returns to his seat to see whether any of the other passengers have a glow attached to their shadows. There is only one halo, and it remains attached to Watson.

Watson hesitates in a meadow of daisies, the white heads, the yellow hearts up to his knees. He breathes in their smoky pollen and coughs. The train has long retreated into the day. Watson walks to the farmer's pond—there is always a farmer's pond—rounds the marshy land until he discovers some rotting boards jutting into the middle of this murky water. He strides down the length of this dilapidated dock. When he reaches the end, he steps over.

Breathes.

Watson breathes thick water into his body, and his lungs protest. They sputter and contract, begin to sink inside his chest cavity. He feels his arms go numb. Watson flings his shoulders out of the water, and heaves his body onto the barely floating wooden dock. Gasps and gasps and gasps.

Sometimes a man needs to half drown in order to find out he's alive at all. Watson is very much alive.

WATSON DERIVES pleasure from each device he brings to life. Aleck proclaims another miraculous idea, and Watson fiddles with metal shavings and glue. With string and long sheets of paper. With inflection. Every week, Aleck requests another impossibility, and Watson produces results out of air. Two tuning forks that vibrate in sympathy. A speaking tube connected to a diaphragm. A human ear.

At first, Aleck cannot bear to touch the thing, severed as it is from a fresh cadaver. So he imagines. He breathes into the shriveled, gray appendage, unsure how to make it register what comes out of his lungs.

Aleck discovers that the membrane of the ear, light as tissue paper, controls the machinations of bones. Build me this, he tells Watson. Make a machine where a paper-thin reed can power its metal components.

Watson nods, continues winding cord along the attic walls and down through the banister of the staircase. When Mabel arrives, she can follow the humming wire with her fingers; a vibrating arrow. When Mabel arrives, Aleck will tell her that the ear is from a run-over pig. Watson, unwilling to hear such nonsense, goes to sleep under the table.

Mabel can't tell for sure, but it looks as if her teacher is shouting into the ear, fluttering indifferently on the workbench. Melly-Melly-Melly, Aleck shouts. Melly-Melly, she sees his lips pronounce.

Oh Aleck: the first ache in her chest.

Mabel wants to reach inside the eardrum and pull out a multilayered kerchief, an egg or a yellow feather. Instead, she points his attention to the pinprick of collapsed skin at the center of the ear's lobe.

A woman, she says to Aleck. She can't hear you.

THE ATTIC HAS BECOME the world. At the very least, a country. Aleck and Watson set up the cities of North America in the loops and crannies of their low-ceilinged existence. They spend their days transmitting messages to hypothetical cities. Watson phones Aleck from Boston to New York; Aleck replies from San Francisco to Los Angeles. They dash from one corner of the attic to another making as many calls as possible. The trick is to encourage the machine's worst problems now. Both shout or yell or sing into the mikes. The cities receive only half a voice. When Aleck sends a message to Portland, a portion of his sentence gets relayed to Detroit. Watson's out-of-tune songs scatter themselves among Miami, Winnipeg, Houston and Yellowstone. They decided that the telegraph apparatus cannot accommodate this new idea of sound that is more than clicks. Their voices splay across this constructed country, they drip their mouths into funneled tubes, they dive their ears toward opposite ends. These frenzied scrambles are their best mistakes.

The two of them perform the victory dance: Aleck's traditional throb of celebration. Hooting and hollering, they crash about the attic, their arms waving above their heads, the chairs around them plummeting. They don't hear their landlady pound on her ceiling. They think the bang, bang, bang is their feet on the wooden floor. They don't hear Mabel arrive for her lesson. Aleck thumps Watson across his shoulders. Watson coughs the names of cities into the air: Grand Forks, St. Louis, New Orleans, Salt Lake City. They point at each other in glee. They hop over wire runners that crisscross the attic floor. They toss quartz and gypsum stones back and forth between them. They stuff their mouths full of fingers and make a popping noise. Mabel can't hear a thing, but she sees two crazy men.

Aleck and Watson exhausted, pleased, dripping with perspiration. We reached L.A. today, they tell her. They point at the map that is the room, that obscenely expands cities, dwindles the rest of the country. Mabel walks from city to city in two steps or less, laughs every time she crosses a state border.

Tag, she shouts when she touches the table that represents New York. Tag, she says to Washington. The final *g* slurs into the back of her throat. Her toes nudge wires. Not It, she declares to the two men. Watson slides his hand across Aleck's tense shoulder. You're It. Aleck joins in, lunges for Mabel.

They play all the rest of the afternoon. Two inventors: chasing Mabel.

13

Platypus Love

THEY BEGAN in the attic. Two men stroking words as if they were parts of a body.

Not my body.

Which had flung itself into a chair at the opposite end of Alex's worktable. I was waiting for my lesson. For my speech therapy. I couldn't touch their fingers or their words. I couldn't decipher a single sentence. The table sliced the room. The attic brimmed with electronic gadgets, wood shavings and other masculine clutter. They began with a verbal agreement that left me out, that also entangled me. The two men held up a model of love across the room, and I reached out. I missed. They promised love from more than one angle. They promised each other.

Two men: voicing a trialogue.

They told a story I couldn't refuse. I can't refuse. But they left me out. Told the story as if I were a character living inside their foregone conclusion.

I turned away. Blanked out the expectations, the geometric possibilities of three. I walked downstairs, announcing my decision to wait in Alex's kitchen. Surely a disciplined and eager student was as important as the toys they tinkered with up there in that bachelor's attic? I turned away from the offer they couldn't even whisper into my mute ears.

I met a boy yesterday in Boston Public Gardens. The day after those two men in the attic offered up their triangular affection. Mother didn't see me slip down to the musky stagnant pond. I sat on wet grass and threw crumbs to the grubby swans our city imports every spring. She assumes I can't speak to anybody new.

I can't speak to anybody new.

But this boy sat next to me and initiated a dialogue. Couple talk. Investing in the power of two. Oh, arithmetic is so much simpler than geometry! He had unusual hands, that boy in the park, twisted and gnarled like an old woman's. He let me stroke them alive. I rubbed the creases between his fingers, charmed his still-emerging calluses. Tingle, he said, you make them tingle, and he opened his hands slowly, stretching each finger. His words brushed against my lips. My eyes inhaled them. And when he smiled, I saw my body's fresh impression beneath me in the grass.

That boy in the park was an equation I could believe in.

But a couple is easy to disrupt. Triangles don't break in half. The pull of that unspoken invitation became too strong a temptation. Those two men, whose words I couldn't grab, spoke to me. The complexities of their story intrigued me. I can't hear promises; I can't hear lies. But I read lips across darkened attic rooms. Those two men, boys really, inserted their hands inside my own, closed their fingers against my palms. Tight. Their lips, loose and suggestive, articulated versions of a trinity.

Whereas the gnarled hand I massaged belonged to only one body.

Mother called and called for me. Of course I heard nothing. My sisters sat far away on another hill and couldn't report her words. She headed home exasperated, knowing I'd soon grow tired of having no one to talk to.

I have no one to talk to.

For that boy in the Gardens, I massaged and massaged, but his body remained singular, his hands only one pair. I clasped my palms together, trapped his one hand between my own two. And there it was: an ending to this beginning.

Now I anticipate a dusty cluttered attic filled with the doubled image of two bodies longing.

That first day, as soon as he noticed I'd deserted his precious attic, Alex returned downstairs, asked me to rehearse speech for him. Whatever I wanted. Say whatever words you feel most comfortable pronouncing, he instructed. I kissed a boy, once, I told him, and left, swinging the gate on my way out. The slam of its metal against wood finished my sentence.

I travel at times with a boy whose name is Odysseus. He lives inside the pages of a book but wants more. I want no less. We sit on the lip of his boat, drag our toes in the slippery green of ocean. We plan feasts of goat's cheese and papayas and fried octopus, which we'll consume when we hit shore. Elixirs we'll drink through crazy straws that bend and twist the fluid into our mouths. I sing to the dolphins and hear them sing back.

Odysseus, though, has a tendency to bind his arms to solid masts whenever he suspects a seditious voice. He taught me about the Sirens and how men drown in their liquid throats. How Sirens use his name as bait to tempt him out of his skin: Odysseus-Odysseus-Odysseus.

A boy on a quest to hear his own name sung and not die in the process. He lashes his body to wood rather than stuff his ears with cotton. The other sailors drown inside a language they can only see. Odysseus claws his own flesh in an effort to consume the treacherous reverberations of female seduction. Then blames his bleeding wounds on mythical beings who are all voice and no body.

Creatures of desire.

Fault lines of pure sensation.

The other sailors ignore his desperation. Bored by his antics, they stuff silence inside their heads, read each other's signs and signals efficiently. Forget him. Odysseus screams on, but none hear. He wants to be converted bit by bit, not devoured whole. He's been trained by the gods to expect devotion. If not from the ship's sailors, then from fish he's schemed into women. I leave him strapped to the ship's mast. Fingernails gouging his rib cage. Praying to the Sirens to release his name from their witchery.

There are two ways to build a triangle, mathematical and mythological. Math requires too much faith for me to follow; numbers are such difficult magic. Mother says too much reading rots your brain, but that's because she was fed poetry that's always a trick or puzzle. Miss-True-the-governess buys me thick books, the heavier the better, and I sink inside their weight. Perhaps Mother does know best, but since I can't hear, what other way is there to rehearse this language? And she does so want me to learn the King's English.

Myth is more reliable than science, although both

come packaged inside the covers of books. Most numbers I've met are imaginary. Places across the world rest side by side on my shelves. The friends I choose live under rocks or beneath lakes or inside someone else's body. I hold hands with Thomas and Alex at the same time, although they will expect me, eventually, to choose.

Eventually is a country I've never been to.

The country I live in is called the bedroom of Boston proper. Boston is made up of parks and slums, Mother says. Boston is made up of rebels and reformers, Father says. Of lovers and the overly cautious, I say.

I indulge a boy who has yet to inherit his own pleasure. Our bodies grasp each other, then depart at strange angles.

I ache for a girl who drops pennies into cracks in the road. She insists such minute treasures shout their own muted acoustics.

I anticipate a boy whose hearing replaces his sight. The double joint of his eyebrows offers me more than just memory. He is his own vision, unfolding.

My lips belong to Alex who stares at them more than my breasts or ankles or wrists. Thomas can have the rest. He demands nothing short of excess. Thomas rubs the tiny triangle of skin just above my earlobe till my kneecaps quiver. He grazes my neck with the tip of his tongue. He strokes my skin so lightly I feel a ripple all the way up my scalp.

Thomas is all cartilage and raised muscle and hair follicles. I creep up behind him while he sleeps, and his body wakes to mine. Before he hears a step. He closes his eyes again, an invitation to stroke his eyelids, to catch his lashes inside the grooves of my index finger.

Alex leaves the room when Thomas and I play these games with our bodies. We two become the undulating current Alex hopes to capture. This isn't dignified, he tells me, but I reject dignified the way Thomas rejects the supremacy of fork tines and gaps over the simple basin of a spoon.

I stand at one point of the triangle, watching the other two. A version of the double. Alex says I live in the center, but he projects a linearity not one of us believes. We believe, instead, in the bent and sweaty contortion of our original geometric figure, flexed equally between three points. I think Alex distrusts equality. Now that these two men have invented the triangle, Alex wants to conflate it back into a smooth line—with those two at each end and me in the middle. Then he can write our story with Thomas as beginning and himself as ending. He doesn't see there is no middle, only space made precious by our joint enclosure.

Will Electric Speech be faster than lipreading? Will I see the telephone flash across computers and highways? These are questions not possible to articulate.

Thomas says that when we die we slip into another body. Those who feel awkward or uncomfortable inside their own skins haven't learned to live with others. I am becoming a specialist of the other. Alex declares Thomas's stories to be preposterous. Alex attends lectures by men preaching a medicine of knives inserted below ribs. A science that ties a deaf girl's hands together with her mother's scarf. His father spent a lifetime transcribing sounds that grow out of our lungs, out of our mouths, but Alex believes words commence at the tip of the tongue. He thinks thoughts reside in the brain. That the body functions only as a useful column for the head. And that nobody lives in Alex's body but Alex.

Thomas believes we're either saints or angels.

Boston, my Boston, for all its advances, will remain faithful to the habit of Oralism. Boston never moves. Only those arriving by water approach Boston with any decency. The city is too trapped in its constructions and reconstructions to recognize the debris collecting in North End Square, in South End, to the west of the Neck. Our city fathers drained the marshes, then left the oyster shells, gravel and street garbage to rot in the sun. Beacon Hill used to be an actual hill till they took off its top. And they poured gravel and street sweepings and oyster shells into Mill Pond. Leveled the surrounding hills to fill the waters north of Causeway Street. Demolished Father's house in the process. At twenty-eight cents a shovelful, men demolished the land's curves, inverted the earth's valleys.

The geologist's sense of time is more spatial than the historian's. Turn down Cow Lane and get lost in a maze of alleys and burnt down shacks from before the great fire. Cross Mystic River Bridge, and the city recedes in fog. Wander past the Bunker Hill obelisk till Winter Street turns into Summer. The distance between Boston and the rest of America is filled with cultural mistrust. Boston is an island located under water. We rarely swim to the surface to breathe. Instead, we trap air bubbles escaping from doomed explorers' nostrils. We have a passion for righteousness. I embrace that passion, though I am deaf to its sermon.

I love the word femur. On my tongue. This is why I lick your leg, and why I lick your leg. I want to taste the murmur within bone. In love with your body wrapped around the hum of this word. And your body. Flesh I embody with my tongue. And with my tongue.

One of you privileges the mind. One privileges the body. Why name you? I am the eager lover of both, that much I know. You worship the body, already a saint. And you, a secular angel, beatific with longing.

You two leave me out. Already. There are two of you, one of me. Convention suggests a *menage à trois* is in my favor, but I know better. Two penises are better than one, you tell me, but you tell me so many lies I can't say which I desire to believe. Every time I reach my palm toward one forehead, I should also touch the other. Otherwise, you tell me, this machine won't function. But I don't think so. We've made this love story in too many directions.

But one of us could disappear, and the other two could continue. Would continue. We've made this triangle so tight, even the loss of one angle wouldn't subtract its energy.

So. We may each be seduced by invisibility, but my desire is ubiquitous. Look: I stroke both hands toward your temples.

There are many rules I'll break but intimacy isn't one. People use sound as a barrier against connection. They say a person's name and then don't have to touch or be touched, though they long for both. That's why you want me to speak. Sound, when it escapes the body, leaves the idea of body behind. And I have left too much of myself behind to settle for a disembodied caress.

I know a boy who rolls marbles under his tongue. Two, three, six, he plops between his lips, sucks back inside his cheeks. Jawbreakers that refuse to melt, slippery against his teeth. Smooth against the inside ridges of his mouth.

The laws of gravity throw objects to the ground before we notice they've abandoned our fingers. Words have a density that hearing people don't recognize. I see them spill from Alex's lips and gather in a puddle at his feet. Thomas is hearing, but he's also Deaf. We rub our arms together in conversations that endure for hours. Skin against skin, our hands rhyme each other's thoughts.

Alex is either hero or thief. The legacy of the hero is a people stronger than their best weakness. The legacy of the thief is loss, the excuse for a lack of precious possessions. Alex will steal the voice of an entire community: a language spoken with arms outstretched. Even a reaching hand frightens Alex with its implication of grammar and syntax. He will steal their language. Only a great thief could perform such a prank. Only a hero.

I taste a boy who sucks lollipops till his lips rainbow. His throat a tunnel breathing sugar. When I lick him my mouth borrows red, blue, mango. I dream ice cream out of his lips. He explodes ice cubes with the simple execution of a smile.

My own eyes lick the air dry. I breathe: in-out, in-out, shallow pockets of oxygen push through my tear ducts. Alex and Thomas play that the world is a toy. They hide countries in the attic and shout messages from one city to another. I never hear what they're saying but witness their laughter when words connect. Thomas has designed a digital counting system, which he demonstrates to me across the room. Alex doesn't see; he shouts out each success and failure, even when his back is turned from me.

He never questions how I manage to gather the score. Between the three of us rest layers of loyalties. Where to begin unraveling? Thomas halts his rampage to hold up three fingers, one bent at the knuckle. I don't want to be so happy I can't remember straining to make my brain hear. I don't want to be content.

Alex bought me a diary for my birthday. He gifts me with pages blank of words.

The body is only as reliable as we expect. My father believes that I emerged—fully formed, perfect even down to the delicacy of my eardrums—out of his forehead. Birth through the vagina for other children.

How does Father explain my loss of hearing? Other senses accompany me, and besides, it's mothers who are responsible for fevers and prolonged delirium. Father says if he'd been with me I never would have caught the scarlet fever that invaded my ears. Father delivered a daughter out of his eye. No wonder I've got perfect vision. No wonder I'm not frightened by malaria or spring fever. But Father never lets himself sneeze in case his body releases an afterbirth.

What I can't hear, I write in my diary. Make nothing into words, make sound visible. I write down "birds" and right away the *b* curls into the shape of a flying animal whose bones are hollow. Alive on the page. Mother says she wakes up mornings on account of singing birds. I don't believe her. I remember singing. Lyrics. *Blackbird sittin in . . .* In church or on the front porch before bedtime. Mama singing in my ear 'cuz that's where words go.

Where words used to go.

Now they just disappear. Till I catch them in my hands and put them on the page. I read faster than

Thomas. We sit on the attic roof, Alex searching for both of us and we read. Same book, same page. We turn each leaf together till I get impatient and rush past. Then I hold the page halfway between its flip and lean into what happens next. Even holding paper between where Thomas is and where I've come to, I get lost. When I'm inside a book, I hear again.

Words in a book travel in straight lines.

It must have been a deaf person who invented writing. The need to see sound. Who else would understand how a person loses herself inside the image of a word? Inside its vision?

Thomas chuckles and I look over the pages dividing us to see where he is. His finger gestures to the word "diaphragm," and I leap two pages back. To singing opera at midnight. Then I remember what hasn't happened yet, and I'm off to the next morning, the pages gathering between us. Thomas will never catch up, he'll never.

The attic roof is all slope and angle. Thomas shows me the opening in the ceiling. Every time we climb up, Thomas says we have to reinvent gravity. Every time we climb up, he says, we create a need for ledges, a need for the temptation to fall. Thomas says he's been falling most of his life, from his childhood into his job as a laborer, from carpentry into mechanics, from electronics into the hands of Alex, the mad inventor.

Except he doesn't say mad inventor. Only I tease Alex about madness and edges. They both assume Alex will be the climax of our story. They have forgotten to trust madness and blurred edges. Thomas loves Alex more than he loves himself. Thomas believes he has already lost, although no contest has been declared.

Truth is, he'd rather lose than win. Thomas wouldn't know how to beat Alex, not even when he's better, so much better, at touch, at knowing when to close his eyes. Alex doesn't trust the world enough to close his eyes except when sleep forces them shut. Nor does he trust his body. Thomas trusts his limbs so thoroughly he never questions their science. He lets his blood pump as fast as it needs to, steps out into the sky when his skin demands blue on blue on blue.

The English language has no proper future tense. But I can pronounce tomorrow. On our wedding night, Alex will offer me a wire from an instrument that mechanically conveys human voice. I will hold in my hand what I cannot hold inside my ears.

Alex carried me on his back today. I am too old for such games, but I ran toward his body and leapt onto his hips, and he embraced my legs in a backward hug. Then he walked forward tirelessly, my chin hooked over his crown. He walked till he reached a hill, then descended. I looked down from a great height with no fear of falling. As long as Alex carries me, I will always be able to see the road ahead. When we returned to the attic, Thomas kissed me on the forehead. He stared at the path I'd just coasted. That kiss, the intersection we three arrive at. An ending of sorts. A beginning. We play the telephone game: I speak into Thomas's ear, Thomas into Alex's and Alex into mine. The game ends there. Sometimes your whole life is decided by a detail. I haven't kissed Thomas again.

I love a boy whose lips were designed by his other lover. Who's kissed and kissed him till his mouth is all anticipation, his longing mere memory. I myself am recovering from a drop of great heights, from a love that I slipped on and that is called falling.

Really, I was thrown.

He crawls inside my damaged arms but won't stay long enough to heal his mind. Or his yearning. I've lost both, of course, for the mind is a paltry substitute once the heart has been stimulated.

Some prefer the loneliness of sanity.

He disappears through the gaps between my fingers, that boy. Wanders lost and upside down in a world that doesn't recognize hunger is an emotion. His want includes his chest and his thighs, but his lips continue to refuse my dialect. Instead, he anticipates the past. He travels to the Arctic, unhinges his tongue from the back of his throat, leaves it to freeze. It lingers there, immobile, awaiting a promised taste of thaw.

And my own body parts?

I have repaired and sewn them back together so often I am all seams. My body a spiderweb of scars. A reminder.

Oh, not of him. Too many lovers have worn through these limbs for any single one to impress my skin with more than a trace of indelible ink. No, the scars testify that once I could be hurt. Once I was whole enough to be broken.

The scars remind me that I used to ignore the ground beneath my feet. And I lament my forgotten talent for stepping—blind—into open air.

I'll marry the boy my father designed for me. Handsome, in love with ideas and soon wealthy from them. A boy who doesn't know his own limitations. Thomas, in love with the idea of Aleck, thinks I make my father's choice. Perhaps I do. The deaf girl and the boy shouting devotion into a telephone receiver. Irony is the invention we all succumb to. When Aleck plays the piano, he expects me to hold my palms against the wood so I can feel sound. He believes he can guess my wants. Really, they are not so contained by rooms and music. My lover's love. The last boy I want.

Alex's hands belong to parlor rooms and piano playing soirees. His veins behave inside his skin. Even weeks and weeks of grease and metal grit and hammer bruises won't convert his fingers to anyone else's phonetics.

Thomas's arms crawl with veins. I rest my palms in the crease inside his elbow and feel the throb of his body pushing outward. His fingers hint at the world. Once I saw Thomas rub the bellyside of his forearm along the bellyside of Alex's. Alex jumped aside.

As if he'd never felt such softness.

Thomas wanted to stroke hairless against hairless, wasn't prepared for Alex's fear. What hasn't been written down is harder for me to believe. Eyes shut, Thomas traces fingernails past the inside of my elbows. Alex leaves the room. His eyes open.

Once he's gone, the stroking ceases. If Alex would close his eyes, he'd see the entire planet strung round and round with standard stovepipe wire, transporting voices. Thomas closes his eyes and sees a trail of discoveries Alex hasn't yet had time for. When I close my eyes, I see the same as when they're open, imprinted on the backs of my lids, instead of on air.

They leave me out, these men with their games. The undersides of my arms are too much like the rest of my body, and predicting the future is a simile for predicting the past. I have no camouflage.

Boston. My Boston. A city cracked with love and left-over corpses. I live in Cambridge: this bridge captured inside a city inside another city. The bridge connects inner and outer. Boston has two faces, one corrupt, one exuberant. The division is one between those who, having sworn off claret, turn finally to whiskey.

Boston's inhabitants become real by wearing a mask. Masks. The only code needed to unlock this city is the code of triumph. That's why Alex is the true Bostonian, and Thomas will forever be a man from Salem. Boston is two cities. And I embrace both.

Alex prefers kisses that begin with his lips closed. Sealed with a kiss, he mouths at me. He takes these catchphrases seriously. Sometimes a moment in a person's life will rhyme with an event gone past. Or one still to come. Thomas kisses me with his whole body.

I used to live in the ocean but grew weary of raw fish and seaweed, of soggy handshakes and slow-motion waltzes. Even the idea of fire can be drowned. In water, it is impossible to remember dust or old age. Most people need to believe in wrinkles, although their reflection frightens. Looking at water from beneath its surface contradicts the possibilities of a mirror. Every time I stared through the ocean's rim out into air another vision of my face evaporated. Narcissus in reverse.

The ocean swallows men whole then spits them back again when women begin a lavish ritual of combing blood from their skulls. Their graying scalps shaved with stones decorated red.

I grew gray hair when I lived in the ocean and emerged from that water with no memory of what I looked like and with a head the color of moon.

Thomas dives into lakes on his days away from the city. Nothing ever catches between his teeth. The trick, he tells me, is not to care. He never closes his mouth or holds his nose, but opens both and lets his body absorb what it will. As long as his lungs are closed, he cannot drown. As long as he locks his lungs shut, the Sirens leave him alone. They want his name but not its container. But what if you *want* to swallow water? I question him. What if catching a mermaid's tale between your teeth is part of the trick? He smiles and repeats: The trick is not to care. Alex sees only container; he doesn't understand the body can be wrapping as well. He stares at my face when I speak and thinks he sees me.

Sometimes he does.

Mostly he witnesses my eyes performing miracles my lips can't fathom. But I am from Boston, and there is always more than one solution to becoming invisible.

I invent a boy who has hair the color of cinnamon. And a body so full of grace I dare not touch him. His mind brims with prairie love and how to swim to China on the back of a horse. I'll find him in books I haven't read yet. Yet: his favorite word. His voice is the length of my bead necklace, and as circular. He rejects the acquisition of knowledge. He says the principals of property and merchandise oppose learning. His mind is too cluttered with broken primary color crayons that he eats like worms and with graphs of the underworld charting the devil's progress as misunderstood bystander.

This boy carries butterflies on the crests of his shoulder blades. He weighs more naked than he does when burdened by the costume of personality and social disguise.

You live inside a book I want to read.

I travel often to when I first meet Alex. He: so expectant, the impulse to teach imprinted on his forehead. Sometimes, I attempt to change the order of my appearance into his life. Or his into mine. I try to meet him in the street instead of that confounded attic, try to meet by accident, instead of Father's prearranged tutoring. I grab his sleeve and whisper my guttural words into his well-tuned ears. But each time I steal into the past, I recognize his face: anticipation. For his brave new deaf girl. For his wife-to-be. Much as I prefer to shake up our story, I am unable to deny him this.

When I travel forward I don't change anything. Why distort tomorrows today? Arrows pointing, tensed to release. My hands reach out to stroke scalp beneath thick strands of hair. Thomas will bow out and Alex will win the lottery. We know this script already, but the two of them never speak, trusting, as they must, in spontaneity. If only there was more at hand than this counter-clockwise chase.

If only Thomas didn't love Alex so much.

They think I'm deaf, but I remember the feel of sound trapped inside my rib cage. I used to eat words when I was a child, before sickness eroded my vocal cords. Before sickness changed other people's hearing. Alex says he likes my voice. He strokes my hair when I speak hesitation. My words stumble and trip over themselves. Alex doesn't ever smile.

Thomas hears me whether I speak or not. The choice is mine. Thomas insists on reincarnation, that we three who are now together will be again. Not necessarily born into the same language. This appalls Alex, the man of science. But Alex doesn't need visions, at least not this one. His voice will live forever.

I hold a girl whose fingertips are fire. She talks with flames that reach from her fingernails to air. She sleeps with buckets of water beside her bed. In the morning, her arms swim in empty buckets. The flames devour the slight hairs on her wrists. On her forearms. I can only believe in her at noon, when the sun eclipses her body's perfect desire.

Thomas has promised to teach me the art of conversation. Skill, he tells me, has nothing to do with it. Patience is a myth. Listening is more about the tilt of the head than about which sounds tickle healthy earlobes. Conversation, Thomas tell me, is a simple conjuring trick of any amateur magician. Pull a word out of a hat, he says, and they'll see a live rabbit.

Those of us from Boston live in two time periods at once. My parents chose the present and some forgotten time buried in thirteenth century England. I live inside the nineteenth and twentieth, but unlike Alex, I'll travel both directions.

I imagine a girl who speaks with both hands. Only the Deaf can understand her. My parents never let me near another deaf child, fearing Dumbness might rub off. Alex, self-proclaimed champion of The Deaf, pushes me in the direction of lips I can't read, ears that can't unscramble the thick words on my tongue. I can't speak this Deaf girl's language, even though her ears rhyme with mine. My parents don't understand: I am more than my disability. And Alex will never see: I am also so much less.

Wherever I wander, speech defines me. Labels other people hang from my skirts. But I know how to live inside a disguise that masks silence. Even a diary is only one clue. The trick to passing as Hearing is to learn as many tricks as possible. Memorize what other people listen to: the scales of a piano, the national anthem. A line of a poem blown back in my face.

I run away from the boy who thinks passion is an apricot pit he could choke on. He bites into fruit gingerly or first splits it open with his fingers. It's not that he doesn't like surprise, he just can't allow himself to rely on astonishment. I used to rub his cheekbones, the bottom of his jaw leading to his chin, kiss the hairs on the back of his neck when he wasn't looking. He thought my passion was aimed at him, but really it was my own body I coaxed alive. My lips wander everywhere except where he fears. He waits for my fingers to abandon his skin so he can turn around and refuse to kiss me.

We climb trees together and hang upside down. Our knees wrap around bark, and our heads brush the grass tips. This boy wants love to be surprising and permanent. Or neither. I don't tell him that you can have no depth without surface, that the air is so thin and stretched here on the surface that breathing becomes dangerous.

So it should be.

My lungs contract and expand, and my blood beats at its own pace. Fast. Even upside down, kisses end up in the belly. But they begin on the stretched surface of skin outlining the mouth. A kiss is neither easy nor expected. Unless you crack it open with your knuckles first. Unless you dissect it before it is born.

Platypus love. Alex and Thomas explain to me that we are a bridge holding hands over water. They discuss the implications of letting go. Men like to believe in drowning as a solution to love. But winter announces itself outside the attic window. The river chokes on ice and snowdrifts. I play with long division and with the buttercups Thomas has stored in Alex's apartment. The river grumbles from below unattached floes that crack its jagged edges. By spring we won't need the yellow blossoms, but for now we cater to their near-invisible petals.

How can you two men not understand that seasons change?

Alex and Thomas play ping-pong on their giant maps. They have cleared all the wires to one side and aim the ball at the center. The trick is not to hit the ball onto the same city twice. They play within, beside, against the rules. Thomas lacks the desire for competition. But Alex can taste the future. He is so close. So close. If they could see beneath my eyelids, they would drop their game, run to embrace me. One in delight. One in fear. Not that my vision is so startling, but uncertainty is one game neither has learned how to embrace. Yet they play on. They play on.

These men will invent the twentieth century.

I prefer to disregard the hierarchy of the apex. A triangle can be a wheel, turning within the turning within. Passion and exclusion and multiplication. And *and* and *and* and *and*.

I laugh with a girl whose hair is plastic snakes braided red, yellow, pink, green, orange. She lives inside the future where she writes books containing pages made from water. I'll meet her, someday, when the path of my remembering and her forgetting cross the same century.

Sometimes, a moment in life rhymes with its future. My father has chosen an appropriate husband; who am I

to say otherwise? My lover would agree. Thomas believes
Alex the better man because he is right and proper and
genius. Thomas appears to me with no flaws except his
own trusting kindness. Alex presumes that when he
speaks a kiss into the telephone I will receive it. In my
future, I will need to fall in love with flaws, with kisses I
cannot hear.

How does the future fit our triangle? A man can go
his whole life without a climax, die in a state of anticipation. But he must believe in phantom rewards, must pur-
sue what he considers eternal compensation.

Most men live inside the climax that just happened,
its echo still throbbing their fingertips. These men lust
after today.

A man who climaxes only once—and early—walks on
a path that leads away from memory. He hopes for a Second Coming to blast away the present. Hope: the emotion rooted in past triumphs. He longs for the explosion
that will release him from his life's extended denouement.

The sun set twice tonight. Once it dipped below the
horizon, and once it disappeared into my mouth. The
first sunset followed nature's law of cycle and expectation;
the second hid from the first but not from me. Both Alex
and Thomas think it is when the sun sets that the moon
becomes possible. But there it is: triumphant in the sky,
hours before the sun risks approaching the lip of horizon.

A woman who climaxes only once has been interrupted.

14

He Swallows the Sound of Sky too Hesitant for Looking

GRAHAM BELL URINATES, PISSING INTO THE WIDE ocean, releasing himself into the element.

Inner tube and water carry the old man away from his dock, through the Bay, toward a gap in shoreline that is ocean. Baddeck Bay, coarse and irritable, allows him to float, just float. He dips one toe into the pebbly water and listens to the grit of minuscule waves against rubber. A sound of scratching. The sound of his body half-immersed in this lake, an inner tube surrounding his legs, cradling his massive neck.

Graham Bell listens.

He leans his head back, back into the water, until the waves stroke his face, then opens his eyes to what lies above him. He discovers sky, matches the straggly clouds above to the fussy waves at his side. If he leans his head to the left or to the right, one ear dips below the surface. One ear reaches toward the underwater sound. If he lies still for long enough, perhaps a microscopic fish will swim into his eardrum.

A person could go deaf that way.

The ripples spin his inner tube round and round. Graham Bell paddles his toes until he faces Beinn Bhreagh.

Until he sees from this distance, his twenty-seven-room castle nestled on his hill. His inner tube has drifted to the middle of the Bay. He is too far out to see his deaf wife inside, sweeping the carpet he brought with him from Scotland. A carpet that belonged to his grandfather. A carpet of colored swirls and implied whooshes.

A carpet that began with the idea of a single thread.

Graham Bell pulls at his chin and detaches a single strand of coarse white beard.

The thick hair loops around his pinkie finger, and he dips it into the ocean. The current catches, loses it again, gradually unwinds his single idea.

A carpet is more about layers of threads woven together than about a singular beginning. A carpet is about the appearance of completion.

The meaning of a word will occasionally worry you, he used to lecture his deaf students, but its sound is constant. And possible. Always remember: Speech is a gift we've been offered. An easy gift. Just open your mouth, reach with your tongue, take what is already there.

His body. What used to be useful has now been forgotten. Graham Bell rubs his hands over his immense belly and finds satisfaction in the dry skin, in his bulk that defies the regular landscape of sea. His hands find his chest, and again he plucks a curly hair. This one pale in his palm. He licks it into the space behind his yellow teeth. There it rests beneath his pink and searching tongue.

He has trapped the sound of it.

He chews the dead skin around his fingers and brings it to life inside the cavern of his mouth. Graham Bell smiles and pushes his body deeper inside the inner tube.

Graham Bell's body is more than the sum of its parts; it is his personality denied. His fingers don't curve around meaning when they touch water; his arms don't translate sound into vision. Only his eyes see; only his ears hear.

Graham Bell has tried not to yell against the vastness. If he were to open his throat and let out sound, the inner tube holding him would toss and twirl and spill the concept of direction all over the bottom of the ocean.

And Graham Bell likes to keep his secrets to himself.

The mind counts even when it sleeps. How many times did he turn over in his sleep? How many times did he snore? Or burp? Or fart? The mind keeps track of the body, but the body has a mind of its own.

His voice is low and dusty. Mabel feels it against her hands. He grumbles at the children, at the dog, at the telephone when it interrupts him for the fifth time this morning. Better to be deaf, Mabel tells him, better to avoid the weary responsibility of hearing. Graham Bell couldn't stop hearing if his life depended on it. Mabel has. He talks and his wife loses the shape of his mouth when he turns to catch an automobile honk behind him. Or he runs away from her in the middle of a word with no clue from him that the word hasn't been completed. Mabel follows his back, trying to see past his incomplete sentence to what notion has driven him into his latest frenzy. But it is only the telephone again. He has to catch it. What a bother, Mabel says when she sees his hand lunge out to capture the voice. Why not just let it ring?

The noise in Graham Bell's ears is not the drone of a fishing trawler beyond the Bay. The noise is not the sky falling into his eyes, his ears, his mouth where he can almost taste the blue. The noise is not the ocean promising him mermaids and eternal lullabies. The noise is a voice generated inside him. Words and sentences, the babble of speaking curls beneath his tongue.

The sky is timid, but Graham Bell is unable to close his eyes against its feeble protest. He cannot speak the words caught beneath his tongue, the words he hears out of his besieged inner ear, his cochlear passage. Words leak into the air so confused he cannot identify one by one by one. One individual hair catches on his tongue. He swallows, chokes and spits the hair back into the ocean.

The inner tube twirls, and Graham Bell sinks his large white head against the reassuring rubber. His body low in the water, his arms and feet hang over the inner tube which has drifted too far out into the Bay for Graham Bell to maneuver his way back again. He has drifted for days. For days. Even nights perhaps. The sun gives no clue. Only the palest promise of daytime. The clouds, like cataracts, fog up his eyes. He lets both hands drop from where they caress his belly into the water and uses them to paddle. When the time comes to return, Graham Bell's hands and toes will have to invent a way back to his castle.

The deaf woman inside will have gone to sleep. He will return in time to kiss her sky-pale skin, her eyelids the color of clouds, her locked lips.

A bug lands on his knee and then washes away. He scrubs, with stubby fingers, the near-transparent skin.

If this inner tube exchanges the air inside for the heavier substance of the surrounding water, Graham Bell will sink. Not even his large body will float him above the waterline. The trick, Graham Bell tells himself, is to believe in buoyancy. He uses his arms as rudders and paddles his toes. The sound of air changing into water is only an illusion. The magician knows how to imitate body language.

The tiny speck in the middle of the Bay that is Graham Bell can no longer be seen from the concealed windows of his castle. A person peering out any one of those twenty-seven windows would not notice the glimmer of bare belly.

The inner tube makes its own way, and Graham Bell's toes wiggle uselessly. The irritating waves lap louder now against the inner tube enclosing his shoulders. The chalky reflection in the water chases his every nod and tremor. Graham Bell is lost in the ocean. His toes squirm there at the end of his legs where he can no longer feel. He is lost in his own body. The beat-beat of the ocean slaps his bare soles.

The memory of chest hair has left a tickle in his throat. Graham Bell is thirsty. He toys with the idea of water distillation, imagines rows and rows of shallow boxes, moisture gathering on their sloping glass tops. Except that would require sunshine, and the sun today has woven itself into a carpet of cirrus cloud. Next, he will notice hunger, and after that the pressing urge to defecate. He shakes his hands free of the salt water and lifts a finger to his mouth. Intends to suck what little moisture may be trapped inside his folds of skin. But there are only more folds, only dry skin. Graham Bell sucks his finger and feels the edge of a nail loosen and detach. He does not spit, cannot afford the moisture loss.

His thirst has become a raging companion.

Graham Bell licks his moustache dry, then regrets the taste of gray on his tongue. His wife sleeps, her lips bare-ly parted, her eyes traveling their inner lids. The roar of ocean enters his body. The broom, transformed from utensil to ornament, hangs upside down on the mantle. The deafening roar of water. Afternoon dust settles on the furniture. He reaches a finger toward the drip of moisture escaping one eye. A medieval castle reconstructed in the twentieth century.

Graham Bell's voice, bellowing, catches inside the inner tube. He cannot hear it. His wife turns over. Her eyes glide rapidly underneath their thin envelope of skin. She dreams a tiny speck in the ocean, an almost audible roar.

Graham Bell closes his gray moustache over his lower lip. Stops noise.

When she wakes from the heat of the stifling summer day, feeling trapped under a colorful quilt crisscrossed with embroidery threads, Graham Bell's wife Mabel will remember only the sound of ringing.

15

The Thought Books of A. Graham Bell

APRIL 3RD, 1922. BEINN BHREAGH

I AM NOW, AND ALWAYS HAVE BEEN, AGAINST laws that will prevent the deaf from intermarrying. Such legal enforcement would in all probability lead to more out-of-wedlock births and less understanding of why the deaf should not congregate. Instead, we should educate deaf children in isolation from each other, promote intercourse with hearing students and not let the deaf gather into groups and societies. When together, the temptation to sign, rather than speak, is too great, and they succumb to this base means of communication. But if a deaf child is immersed in the hearing world, grows up speaking and lipreading, he will be as abhorrent of manual communication as is my dear wife Mabel. By choosing a hearing man as her husband, she left behind forever, at the tender age of seventeen, a disabled, and disabling, world. To the extent that she fears its pull even today.

Tho' I plead with her, Mabel will not enter into conversation with other deaf ladies, even those who, like herself, have been afflicted with deafness late enough in life to remember the drama of speech. And when I bring the parents of deaf mutes home, she finds herself unable to perform the sentences they need to hear, to convince them that I know their child's best interests.

Mabel fears my efforts to maintain an association with the deaf.

I have given up showing her off altogether, tho' it pains me that the world might not recognize Mabel as the deaf wonder she truly is. At night, to coax me away from my measurements and calculations, she promises to whisper difficult phrases directly into my ear.

Glacier. Truncated. Public address system. Monolithic. I do not always understand her pronunciation as her speech blurs more each year. So, I find myself working later and later on my experiments. Until I have reversed day and night, and travel through dawn in slumber.

MAY 28TH, 1922. BEINN BHREAGH

I HAVE KNOWN evil degenerate men in my time, but they are far outnumbered by the perversely obstinate Sign Language supporters who encourage deaf people to congregate, educate themselves and intermarry. Idiots! Do they not understand the danger of allowing a defective population to grow in number? Or do they not care? My life's work has been making things— dogs, machines, deaf children—speak, yet these antiquated humanitarians refuse to acknowledge the benefits I have offered humanity, accuse me of being a rabid oralist, continue to support schools and laws which favor public, manual communication. If only they would listen!

Tho' they gave me a scarce two minutes, I once convinced the Senate, with letters procured from principals of all schools begun by my method, to reverse the House decision to provide funds for teacher training at Gallaudet. I knew they would allocate the money to deaf graduates of their own institution. Instead, such government support should promote articulation, not only in deaf, but in hearing schools as well, to preserve the purity of the English tongue. Were he alive, Grandfather would be outraged to hear this language so deteriorated by the influx of foreign contamination.

What deaf child who can talk easily and effectively with his fingers will make the laborious and strenuous effort to twist his tongue in a manner it has not learned naturally, to read the ghosts of words on strangers' lips? We must force the gift of speech into their mouths, down their throats: otherwise we deprive them of normal existence. We must separate them so they are not tempted to talk or laugh or fall in love with each other.

Thomas Gallaudet and his son have always claimed their school to be a success. Most of their students—waving the air frantically and writing down what they need to say—graduate to become bank clerks or newspaper employees or teachers. It is clear as a bell that the object for the education of the deaf-and-dumb is to fit them into this world of hearing–speaking people, *not* to let them get away with scribbling English equivalents of their own language onto bits of paper. Such a fantasy of independence will only create a separatist community and will lead the deaf child away from the goal of communication back toward silence.

JUNE 2ND, 1922. BEINN BHREAGH

MY BEST STUDENT, George Sanders, has become my worst failure. He has never mastered adequately the art of speech and lipreading, and he insists on marrying a deaf girl, tho' it seals his silent entombment. George's father believed in my abilities, promoted me to his friends and politicians, and paid my inventor's wages. Yet today, George claims his disabilities to be of social rather than medical causes. His children, tho' they be healthy and whole and hearing, speak to him with their hands and their faces. At family gatherings, the entire room will be silent but for the undulating air surrounding their arms. Friends and relatives and even spouses all speaking with their mouths tightly closed.

George embraces the deaf community as if such a community existed. As if it were his very own.

JUNE 3RD, 1922. BEINN BHREAGH

I USED TO BELIEVE her arms were pure cream.

Marie.

I want to kiss her entire face, lick her belly, suck on each—perfect—toe, tie her up, blindfold her, make her return to me. Come back.

Mabel holds herself away from me, and I do not question why. Who can live easily with an animal who dreams day into night, night into day? I used to dream I might cure her deafness. We used to believe that together.

Mabel, before we were married, would come to the attic where Watson and I tinkered with wires and bells and electric currents hours before her lesson. Her eyes, sharp as a whistle, missing nothing. Watson, too embarrassed to speak with this prize student of mine, would point and nod and grin over our tiny contraptions. And Mabel, for my sake, would pretend to understand his weird gestures. Often, I would rush home from my classes in anatomy or electrical science to find the place deserted. The two of them off on some rooftop, catching the atmosphere between their hands.

Children, both.

I look at my daughters today and see that same girl. Except these hear and will heed my call. Their husbands will step into the roles of sons. They will carry on my name and spirit in every manner except the birth certificate. It is better so. Am I not more Gardiner Greene Hubbard than he himself? So will my sons-in-law become me and my ideas. Mabel, tho' she has accepted the use of my name, remains individual in her heart. She reads more and more each day, and talks less. What can this mean?

Mabel chose me, in the end, not I her. I wanted her father's name and sturdy backing and the eager student that she then was. What did she want of me, I wonder. And what did she get?

JUNE 6TH, 1922. BEINN BHREAGH

MARIE KEPT her hands covered by gloves because they were darker than thought proper at the time. Why do I only know this now, so many years behind the fact? Mabel refuses the convention of gloves altogether, flaunting her brown and wind-cracked skin to whichever eyes can keep up with them. They are never still, Mabel's hands, but dart and flirt through the air as if they have a life of their own. When I am just waking, Mabel will enter my bedroom and scratch my dry and yellowing whiskers, rub oil deep into my chin and neck. This pleasure makes my skin ache.

What wonders would Marie's hands have performed with such oils?

JUNE 22ND, 1922. BEINN BHREAGH

THE LAND and the weather are so much more punishing here in Canada. Yesterday, I witnessed a hailstorm. I choose the word *witness* because, with the smashing down of ice chunks the size of rocks, I was awed by the destructive Nature that controls us by fear and danger. This world is but a feeble construction of lies and fallacies. Windows are smashed and the coverings of horsecars ripped to tatters. Tho' it is summer, hot frozen pellets of white water are strewn across the streets. In town, a small child got knocked to the ground by the force of one hailstone. Its mother knelt there beside its unconscious body. Perhaps, after all, I should have studied medicine. For the woes of the world are many, and this tinkering I do in my laboratory yields only voices—multiple and of varying degrees of loudness—and piles and piles of notebooks filled with dates and neat columned figures.

I called out to Mabel, but she could not hear me above the din of hailstones—battering against the roof as if it were my body.

JULY 14TH, 1922. BEINN BHREAGH

I HAVE BEGUN to get letters, in recent years, from deaf men and women who feel the need to blame me for unhappy lives arising from their unfortunate condition. As infants, many of these people were sterilized by doctors attempting to purify humankind. These letters blame such decisions on my Memoirs and pamphlets wherein I stated that the deaf-and-dumb, where possible, should be eliminated from the human stock. I have always deprecated legislature interfering with intermarriage of the deaf. This is not the way to prevent their congregation. Rather, we should encourage unions between deaf and hearing people, as my wife's parents have done. The sterilization of deaf babies begs the question of whether these infants were born deaf or became so through sickness or disease. My own dear wife had no congenital flaw, her only fault being that she contracted scarlet fever as a young girl. Do these deaf fanatics believe I wish her to be sterile and myself childless?

Furthermore, these letters accuse me of inventing the one device that, more than any other, separates the deaf from the hearing world. Blasphemy!

THE DAYS BEGIN to shorten, tho' imperceptibly. The lawn is littered by fly-covered rinds of lemon peels. In one day, I consume an entire sack of this fruit. By late evening the sun has dipped below the horizon and the Bay shimmers crimson, the moon a low scarlet: reminder of what the day has been.

Of what my day has been.

Forty-six years ago, I achieved glory with that greatest of all nuisances: the telephone. And have continued inventing ever since: induction balance, intermittent-beam sounder, vacuum jacket. Kites.

The most true creation is that of a speaking deaf.

Mabel offers me tea and sugar with her mouth, biscuits and chocolate with her tongue. Wisteria and hibiscus held out to me by her teeth. What poison, drunk down as an elixir, pools in her throat and larynx?

Afternoons, when I can barely breathe from the heaviness of this salt atmosphere, and my eyelids clamp shut in protest, Mabel comes to me with fresh-cut cucumber skins and buries their coolness into the crevices that used to be my body. Tho' her ears be defective, her mouth and hands offer sympathetic vibrations to soothe what ails an old man.

WASHINGTON HAS ALWAYS BEEN my true city, tho' I plan to be buried here on my vast land. And Mabel beside me. When we moved to the District of Columbia, Hubbard purchased for our sake a mansion. Not quite the size of what we've built here but the most enormous house in Washington at that time. Ninety-nine thousand dollars! Every fashionable room imaginable to a high society, including a stable with modern steam-heated rooms for our dozen or so servants. Living there, Mabel thought I might miss the opportunity to vote, but I was, on the contrary, relieved. What do I know of Republicans or Democrats? I love the whole human race but can never decide about individuals. Here in Canada I find peace from the nagging politicians. I am an American citizen and deem it my duty to abstain from all participation in Canadian politics.

Here, Mabel indulges me in my twenty-four-year-old hobby of sheep breeding. I will let live only six-nippled twins. The rest I donate to charities for picnics. I should have become interested in inherited longevity much sooner: the eugenics movement has successfully led to the sterilization of undesirables and to laws restricting immigration—how else to ensure selected breeding?—and it may yet improve the human race. Too late for me.

AUGUST

MY LIFE between the telephone and now seems not to have happened. I struggled so hard to conceive it in Brantford and deliver it in Boston. The argument of national ownership goes on. Somehow I either snapped my fingers once too often or invoked an ancient Melly-incantation. Or simply couldn't hear the machine that is Progress. Each year, after the telephone, has disappeared. Time consumed into what remains here: a drawer full of unfiled patents and a laboratory of failed gadgets. What used to be ideas.

A watery life, now evaporated.

Look, Mabel, my arms are more wrinkled than the surface of the ocean, tho' the wind is enough to cause goose pimples to sprout across my exposed skin. My feet, peeking through their sandals, show spots of reverse freckles, white blotches that increase in size whenever the sun burns down. I used to own a fluid body but have become dust, held together by sheer will.

When we moved to Washington, I opened a day school for the congenitally deaf, several boys whose tuition fees paid for their private tutors and articulation instructors. Tho' I claimed so at the time, it was not the vanishment of Visible Speech from every school's curriculum which led to the school closing in under a year. The truth is, tho' I shudder to write it, the congenitally deaf cannot be taught to hear.

The dragonflies this far north are tinted entirely blue and fly about, one mated to another. When I listen, I hear no sound but the propeller flutter of their wings.

I hear no sound.

No.

16

Sympathetic Vibrations

KITES IN THE BELL MUSEUM IN BADDECK INCLUDE Hargrave box kites, Oriental kites with long heavy tails, kites with no tails at all, Graham Bell's cygnet, the Siamese twins, Mabel II, beeswax and celled kites. Kites, finished and photographed black and white against a gray maritime sky, represent a version of flying.

Wednesdays, the museum staff hold kite-making and kite-flying lessons.

Graham Bell's giant ring kite reaches thirty feet in diameter and requires twelve men to lift it. The breeze catches between its hundred spokes and transforms the kite into a ferris wheel that has been released from gravity.

In 1906, Graham Bell's valet wakes him with the news that his first grandson was safely born (his own sons all stillborn or died in infancy). His immediate exclamation— but can he fly?—Graham Bell later justifies by explaining he'd been dreaming of kites.

A LOCAL WASHWOMAN RECALLS PROFESSOR BELL:

MAKING PEOPLE TALK from a long way off! And by means of an iron box and a coil of wire. Stuff and nonsense. Heaven knows there are plenty of folks at a distance I'd just as soon not talk to at all.

CLOSED CAPTIONS:

THE DESIRE TO IMITATE human speech reaches as far back as the Bible, as far forward as science fiction computers.

In the *Book of Job*, God asks: Canst thou send lightenings, that they may go, and say unto thee, Here we are?

The Oracles of Delphi speak their prophecies through funnels whose narrowed tips peek from the temple walls.

The string telephone is popular in Persia, China and Ceylon long before the Europeans copy its design.

When his telephone first becomes popular, Graham Bell suggests *Ahoy* as the greeting when one picks up the receiver. T. Edison suggests *Hello,* Gaelic for *Holy Be Thou,* is more appropriate.

On New York City's Broadway Street in 1880, more than 350 overhead telephone wires are visible.

United States President Garfield remarks that it used to take all day to get the bad news, but with the invention of the telephone, he could get it right away. When Garfield is shot, Bell rushes to the hospital because he has developed a new contraption that detects metal. No one considers the metal coils lurking inside the hospital bed, and Garfield dies while Bell sets and resets his machine.

Early telephone operators, always female, are required to wear a six-pound harness headset for the duration of their work shifts. Their necks lean to one side from the sheer weight of the contraptions.

Voice transmission over early telephones is so poor that the operators act as translators, relaying messages from the caller's mouth to the receiver's ear.

At first, callers tap their telephone machines with a pencil to alert the receiver to an incoming call. Watson, though, soon invents a *thumper* then *buzzer* then the *bell* we still hear today.

The world record for the number of people squeezed into a telephone booth is eighty-eight.

The present day football huddle, a sports tradition, begins at Gallaudet School by deaf players who wish to pass on plays and tactics without the opposing team "overhearing."

Bell laboratories conceives the technology for the M-9 gun.

The final telephone advance Graham Bell is alive to behold is the dial telephone. Touch-tone "dialing" appears after his death.

ASL, like any language, begins in the body. Muscle by muscle, the speaker moves out toward the recipient, a lover with arms open.

FAX machines transmit the written word through telephone lines.

E-mail, an electronic system of computer communication, travels through telephone modems.

At the time of their deaths, T. Edison, who is partially deaf, holds over 1300 patents; Graham Bell holds five, none of which mention the telephone.

After successfully inventing the telephone, Graham Bell:
  – develops two new breeds of sheep
  – suggests a sound detector for locating icebergs
  – invents the action comic strip
  – sets up his two sons-in-law as president for the American Genetic Association, and editor for the National Geographic Society.

In 1932, *National Geographic* insists on the Bell name for an Arctic island.

In 1492, he sailed the ocean blue. . . . Columbus, when the Americans first discover him on their land, refuses to believe that the "noise" they make with their tongues and lips is "speech."

Modern telephones are shaped like shoes, baskets of fruit, race cars, ducks, sports equipment, pianos.

In 1755, Abbé de l'Epée opens a school for the deaf in France. A quarter century later, twenty such schools exist in Europe.

Shortly after Laurent Clerc brings his teaching methods to the U.S., almost half the teachers at his Gallaudet school are deaf.

The latest hearing aid, the Cochlear Implant, is made of twenty-two distinct electrodes threaded under the skin inside a deaf person's ear. This person also wears a microphone connected by a thin wire to a sound processor. Deaf adults have difficulty adjusting to this device, which approximates the voice of Donald Duck. Young children implanted with this device have more success accepting such bodily intervention. They haven't yet shared the cultural memory of imposed communication. Some successfully use the Cochlear to hear through the telephone.

In 1880, the Congress of Educators of the Deaf meets in Milan to vote on whether deaf students will be taught in their own language. It goes without saying, Graham Bell feels the need to stand up and say, that those who are themselves unable to speak are not the proper judges of the value of speech to the deaf. Oralism wins the day, mainly because deaf teachers are excluded from the vote.

By 1900, the ratio of deaf teachers in schools for deaf students has been reduced to 25%. By 1960, it has dropped to 12%.

The invention of the telephone continues to this day.

A LOCAL BOATMAN RECALLS PROFESSOR BELL:

HE GOES UP THERE on sunny afternoons with his thingamajigs and fools away every blessed day. Flying kites. He has dozens of them—all kinds of queer shapes—and they're but poor things, god knows! I could make better myself. And the men that assist him—grown men—go up there and spend the livelong day. Flying kites.

The greatest foolishness I ever heard.

BY THE TIME Aleck has successfully invented the telephone, every school but one teaches Oralism and Oralism only.

More and more, Mabel Bell internalizes the memory of hearing. She no longer resorts, as she did when younger, to the pretense of mishearing. Poetry becomes her way of digesting the world. She loves the visual rhymes she can recognize on the page. Her favorite poetry is Ovid's *Metamorphoses*, whose physical transformations engage her sensual cravings.

Reach out and grab each word, a stone in your mouth: what he used to tell Mabel when he was still her teacher.

Graham Bell, a millionaire because of his gadget, encourages Oralism and financially supports laws that will prohibit Sign Language by deaf people. He wants to ensure such children don't grow up abominations. He says he invented the telephone to cure the deaf.

I want to invent the sound of a lover's voice a hundred miles away, he once told Mabel. He believes he has achieved this invention.

Sometimes, your own lips betray you.

CREDITS

ALTHOUGH THE CHARACTERS IN THIS NOVEL are based on historical people, the characterizations and events are fictional and should be read as such.

I am indebted to the following texts for much of my research and information about Alexander Graham Bell and his times:

Aitken, William. *Who Invented the Telephone?* London: Blackie and Son, 1939.

Bruce, Robert. *Bell: Alexander Graham Bell and the Conquest of Solitude.* New York: Cornell University Press, 1990.

Costain, Thomas. *The Chord of Steel: The Story of the Invention of the Telephone.* New York: Doubleday & Company, 1960.

Lane, Harlan. *When the Mind Hears: A History of the Deaf.* New York: Penguin Books, 1984.

Toward, Lilias M. *Mabel Bell: Alexander's Silent Partner.* Toronto: Methuen, 1984.

Watson, Thomas. *Exploring Life: The Autobiography of Thomas A. Watson.* New York: D. Appleton and Company, 1926.

As well, I would like to acknowledge Leonard Cohen for his creation of the Telephone Dance in *Beautiful Losers* (New York: Viking Press, 1970), which appears here in Chapter Eight: "Naked in Your Body."